THE CHANCE OF A LIFETIME

Lisa clutched her portfolio and looked at the sign on the office door. It read WILLOW CREEK GAZETTE. Her knees felt weak. She took a deep breath as she opened the door.

"Mr. Teller?" she asked timidly. "It's Lisa Atwood."

"Come sit down," Mr. Teller said with a smile. "Now, tell me about this idea of yours."

"It's about horses," she began. "See, I ride at Pine Hollow. A lot of other kids in town do, too. It's a very busy place. There's so much going on for young riders that I think you should have a column about it in your paper. I have a lot of writing experience," she continued a little breathlessly. "The name of the column is 'Hoof Beat.'"

Mr. Teller leaned back in his chair. "Deal," he said. "I want five hundred to seven hundred and fifty words a week. I'll pay you fifteen dollars a column. Think you can have your first column to me by next Wednesday?"

For fifteen dollars, she'd turn it in that afternoon! Lisa practically floated down the stairs. She was a reporter! This was the most exciting thing that had happened to her since she'd discovered horseback riding.

THE SADDLE CLUB

HOOF BEAT

BONNIE BRYANT

A BANTAM SKYLARK BOOK®

NEW YORK · TORONTO · LONDON · SYDNEY · AUCKLAND

RL 5, 009-012

HOOF BEAT

A Bantam Skylark Book / February 1990

A special thanks to Miller's Harness Company for their help
in the preparation of the cover. Miller's clothing and accessories
are available through approved Miller's dealers throughout the
country. Address Miller's at 235 Murray Hill Parkway, East
Rutherford, New Jersey 07073 for further information.

ISBN 0-553-15780-9

Published simultaneously in the United States and Canada

PRINTED IN THE UNITED STATES OF AMERICA

CWO   0 9 8 7 6 5 4 3 2 1

For Nancy Kaplan Mansbach, cofeature editor
and fellow LULLA winner

"EASY, BOY," CAROLE Hanson said, patting the black foal's neck gently. Samson eyed Carole warily, then glanced at his mother, Delilah, who stood nearby.

Carole held a halter in her hand. She showed it to the foal. He looked at it curiously, but there was no fear in his eyes. This was the third day in a row that Carole had brought the halter to the fence by his paddock. She thought he was ready to try it on.

Although Carole was only twelve, she was an experienced rider. With Samson, she hoped to become an experienced trainer as well. Samson had been born at Pine Hollow Stables, just a few months before. Carole and her best friends, Stevie Lake and Lisa Atwood, had been present at the birth. It had been one of the most exciting experiences they'd ever had. It was hard to believe, even now, that the fine strong foal who stood next to Carole had once been the scrawny newborn, struggling to stand up and take his first sip of milk. He'd grown tremendously in the first months and could now run around the paddock he shared with his mother for long periods of time. Still, he was just a baby, Carole thought with a smile. Every time she stepped into the paddock, the little foal ran to hide behind his mother's tail.

Stevie and Lisa stood by the fence outside the paddock. Lisa held Delilah on a lead rope. The girls knew that if the mother stood still, the foal was more likely to stand still as well. Stevie and Lisa held their breaths while Carole put her arm over Samson's neck to place the halter on his head.

The three girls were accustomed to working together. They'd become best friends at Pine Hollow and had formed The Saddle Club. The club had only two rules. The first was that members had to be horse crazy. That was easy for them. The second rule was that they had to be willing to help one another. Since there was always plenty going on, they'd worked together a lot.

Carole was the most experienced rider. She'd been brought up on Marine Corps bases where, as a colonel's daughter, she had taken riding lessons all her life. She was determined to spend the rest of her life with horses, as well.

Stevie, the only girl in a family of four children, had started riding so she would have something to do that was different from anything her brothers did. She worked hard at her riding and she was very good—as long as she wasn't in trouble with Max, the owner of the stable. Stevie had a knack for practical jokes and getting into hot water and frequently seemed to lead her friends right into it with her!

Although Lisa, at thirteen, was the oldest of the trio, she was the newest to horseback riding. She had started only a few months before and had begun riding because her mother thought it was something every proper young lady should know *something* about. Mrs. Atwood hadn't been prepared for the fact that, after her first lessons, Lisa had wanted to learn *everything* about it. When Lisa discovered how much fun riding was, and when the three girls had formed The Saddle Club, Lisa had somehow found the courage to tell her mother she wanted to give up some of the other "proper young lady" activities her mother had insisted upon, like painting, ballet, violin, and needlework. Mrs. Atwood hoped this was a temporary situation, but Lisa knew better. Her mother was no more enthusiastic about Lisa's horseback riding than she was about her daughter's straight-A report cards. Mrs. Atwood didn't think proper young ladies *needed* straight A's.

"Okay, boy," Carole spoke softly, "here we go." She stood by the foal. Although she knew the foal could not understand her words, she wanted to keep him calm with her tone of voice. Samson stood still. She laid the nose strap of the halter across his muzzle.

He pulled back quickly. Carole stood her ground. She touched his muzzle with the leather once again. This time, Samson didn't pull back. She removed it. He stood still. She looked over toward the fence, wanting reassurance from her friends.

"You're doing fine," Lisa said. "He's ready. I can see it in his eyes."

Carole patted the foal once again. Then, while talking to him softly and confidently, she slipped the halter around his muzzle and drew the crown strap up behind his ears. She had it buckled before Samson knew what was happening.

The foal shook his head, trying to rid himself of the halter. It didn't budge. That made him shake all the more. He looked to his mother for help. She only glanced at him, then turned her attention to the sugar lump Lisa held for her.

"Good boy," Carole said. "That's it. That's all there is to it. Good boy," she repeated. She tried patting him, but he was shaking his head too vigorously to notice.

Carole thought that was enough for the first day. As quickly as she'd put it on, she removed the halter. Samson shook his head a final time, then discovering the odd feeling had gone, he turned his attention to his mother's udder. He was ready for some lunch.

Lisa released Delilah's lead rope. Carole climbed the fence quickly and the three of them watched the horses together.

4

"That was really neat," Lisa said. "Everybody should be able to see that kind of thing happen."

"If everybody came here to see it happen, it wouldn't be so special for us," Stevie said. "We wouldn't be able to get our front-row seats, would we?"

"No, I don't want everybody here," Lisa said thoughtfully, rolling up the lead rope as she spoke. "I just wish everybody could understand the experience—share in it, you know? Like, I think it would be great to be able to write about that kind of thing and let people know how it feels to be with horses."

"Well, maybe," Carole said dubiously. "Except that I'd never be able to describe it."

"Some people can," Lisa argued, following Carole into the stable. "There are a lot of great writers who would know just exactly what to say."

"But they weren't here," Stevie reminded her. "So, now, it's just us who know what it was like to watch Samson have a halter on for the first time."

Lisa slung the looped rope over her shoulder and led the way back to the locker area where they would change their clothes. She thought she could still feel her heart beating with the excitement of the scene— the first training of a foal. It *had* been exciting. Why *couldn't* that experience be shared?

"Ooh, pee-yew," Stevie groaned, entering the locker area. "I just hate the smell of paint, don't you?"

Carole wrinkled her nose. "Sure," she agreed, "but it's got to be done." Carole could be very matter-of-fact sometimes.

Stevie peered into the tack room where the paint smell originated. "What a disaster area!" The floor was scattered with saddles, bridles, halters, and spare parts. The walls were freshly white.

"Maybe we should offer to help put the stuff back," Carole suggested.

"You don't have time," Stevie reminded her. "You promised to sell tickets at the shopping center for the library raffle today and tomorrow, remember?"

Carole's jaw dropped. "Oh, no!" she said. "I'd forgotten all about it."

Stevie smiled at her friend. "You always forget everything, unless it has to do with horses, don't you? That's one of the reasons you keep me around—to remind you, right?" she kidded Carole.

Carole sat down on the bench and removed her boots. "I can't believe I forgot about that! The problem is—" She paused and crinkled her nose in concentration.

"I bet we can help," Lisa said brightly. "Whatever it is."

"Maybe you can," Carole conceded. "The problem is that I'm supposed to be there all day tomorrow so I won't be able to work with Samson. Today's lesson should be reinforced right away."

"That's no problem at all," Stevie said quickly. "Lisa and I can do that. All we need to do is to get the halter on for a few seconds, right?" Carole nodded.

Lisa slipped out of her riding clothes and into her

street clothes. Stevie and Carole chatted about the library raffle. The first prize was two weeks at Moose Hill, a sleepaway riding camp. All three of them had daydreamed about going, but it seemed unlikely that their parents would go for it. They'd already been on two trips this summer—to a dude ranch and to New York City! Stevie said she wanted to buy all the raffle tickets, then realized that she didn't have any money.

Normally, Lisa would have joined in the conversation, but just then, Lisa's mind was on something else. She couldn't stop thinking about Samson's first training lesson and how much she thought other people would enjoy learning about it. She smiled, remembering.

"Say, dreamface," Stevie said, noticing Lisa's faraway look. "What's on your mind? You planning to go to Moose Hill by yourself?"

"Oh, no. I was just thinking about Samson," Lisa said. "It was just so much fun to be a part of his first lesson. Everyone should be as lucky as we are! It's news that people should get to hear about."

"News, news," Stevie echoed, then her face lit up. "That reminds me. I've got some news! I can't believe I forgot!"

"Well?" Carole prodded, pulling on a pair of gold cotton shorts.

"What is it?" Lisa asked. Stevie sounded excited and Lisa had learned long ago that when Stevie was excited about something, it was usually something neat, even when it meant trouble.

"I'm going to have a sister!" Stevie announced.

"Your mother's—?" Lisa began, stunned. It wasn't so long ago that she'd thought her own mother was going to give her a baby sister or brother. She hadn't been excited at that prospect at all!

"Oh, no!" Stevie said, giggling. She pulled her T-shirt over her head and started to tuck it into her denim cutoffs, then changed her mind. She left the shirt untucked. "Not a baby. What I mean is that this girl, Trudy something, is going to stay with us for a couple of weeks. She'll be like my sister because she's just about our age, and finally I'll have an ally against all those brothers of mine!"

"Hey, now *that's* news," Lisa said enthusiastically. "Is she some kind of foreign exchange student or something?"

Stevie shoved her boots to the back of her cubby and crammed her riding clothes into a zipper bag. "If you call Washington a foreign place, then yes," Stevie said. "See, her mother works with my mother in D.C., and her parents won this trip to Hawaii, but it's only for two. Her mother was going to give it up because they couldn't take Trudy, but Mom invited Trudy to visit us. Her mother said she's never been to the country before. Can you imagine?"

"Sure I can imagine," Lisa said. "After all, except for the American Horse Show in New York City, it's not as if we've spent much time in the city, is it? I think it would be weird living in a city, and I bet Trudy will find it weird living with you."

"I just hope she isn't too weird," Stevie said. "After all, it's going to be my only chance to have a sister."

"I didn't mean that it would be *Trudy* that's weird," Lisa said, pursing her lips so Stevie wouldn't see her smile.

"You think *I'm* the weird one?" Stevie challenged.

Lisa couldn't hold her giggle. Stevie joined her. Stevie *was* a little weird, but it was a nice weird as far as her friends were concerned.

"Carole, your shirt's on backward," Stevie said, changing the subject as she watched her friend pull down the ends of her polo shirt.

Carole looked down, confused. "I could have sworn . . ."

"You know," Stevie teased, "maybe you ought to wear shirts with pictures of horses on them. Then you'd always put them on right."

"Ha, ha." Carole grinned, then shook her head. "The trouble is, you're right. I am a total flake. Who knows what I'll do next?" She jammed her hands into her jeans pocket. "Oh, no," she said, genuine distress in her voice.

"What's the matter?" Lisa asked.

"Where's the money?" Carole began. She reached to the bottom of her pockets and wiggled her fingers in vain. "My dad's birthday-present money . . ."

"You're getting him some tapes, aren't you?" Stevie asked.

Carole nodded. Her father was crazy about things from the fifties and sixties. She'd been saving for a while to get enough money to buy him some old record albums he particularly wanted.

"In your riding pants?" Lisa suggested.

Carole searched the pockets of her breeches, but the money wasn't there. "It's fifteen dollars! I can't lose it. His birthday's only a couple of weeks away. If I . . ."

"How about your wallet?" Stevie suggested. "Where is it?"

"Oh, that's in this pocket," Carole said, tapping her rear pocket. "But Dad's birthday money isn't there. See, if I kept it there, I'm afraid I'd forget that it's special money and I'd spend it."

"Your bag?" Lisa asked.

Carole tore the clothes out of her backpack, but there was no money there. She sat on the bench, put her elbows on her knees and her chin in the palms of her hands. She frowned, trying to think hard. "The last time I saw it, I had it in my hand. I remember that. I just don't remember what I did with it."

Lisa felt awful for Carole. There was nothing she could do. Carole just *was* forgetful and a little flaky. This wasn't the first time she'd forgotten something important. Lisa recalled the time Carole had almost left her clothes and sleeping bag behind when they'd gone on an overnight trip.

"I sometimes carry money in my shoes," Stevie suggested.

"That's it!" Carole said, brightening. "It's in my boots." While her friends watched, Carole reached into the toe of her right riding boot. "Got it!" she said, and pulled out two crumpled bills, a five and a ten.

"Carole!" Stevie said. "That's no way to treat money—especially big money like that."

"I know," Carole sighed. "But I just have to find a place to stash it until I can get to the mall to buy the records for Dad." She looked at Stevie. "You helped me find it," she said. "Will you help me keep it?"

"Of course," Stevie agreed. "If you really want me to."

"That would be great. Then you hold on to it for the next three weeks. I'm going to the mall the Saturday before his birthday. Give it to me then." Carole slapped the money into Stevie's hand. "Don't give it to me before then no matter how much I beg, okay?"

Stevie looked at the money and then looked at her friend. "Are you sure?" she asked. Carole nodded. Slowly, Stevie took out her own wallet, lifted the flap to a hideaway compartment behind the billfold portion of it, closed the flap back over the money, and tossed her wallet back into her backpack. "Don't worry that it's going to be mixed up and confused with *my* money," Stevie said. "All I've got is four cents and nobody's going to mix up your fifteen dollars with my four cents."

"I know that," Carole said. "I trust you. Besides, you only ever have four cents! I'd better run. Thanks. See you both!"

With that, Carole picked up her things and practically ran out the door.

"You know, there are a lot of exciting things happening," Lisa said to Stevie as she finished putting her things neatly into her cubby. "Between Samson's training and your new 'sister,' there's a lot of news at the stable."

"Sure, I can just see the headlines in tomorrow's paper," Stevie said sarcastically.

Lisa thought it was all in the way you looked at it, and the way *she* looked at it gave her an idea. A *great* idea, she thought, with a secret smile.

2

LISA CLUTCHED HER portfolio so tightly that she was sure she was crumpling the papers inside. She looked at the sign on the door. It read WILLOW CREEK GAZETTE. Her knees felt weak. She took a deep breath. It didn't do anything to make her knees feel better. She knocked on the door anyway.

"C'mon in!" a gruff voice responded from inside.

She opened the door and peered around it.

What she expected was something like *The Daily Planet* city room—a sea of desks, each with its own computer screen and keyboard, most being operated by frazzled and dedicated reporters, determined to tell the truth to the news-hungry people of Willow Creek.

What she *saw* was something different. There were three desks. Each looked as if it had been rescued from the junk pile. One did, actually, have a computer on it. One of the others had an old-fashioned desktop manual typewriter. The third may have had a typewriter on it, but Lisa couldn't be sure. It was piled too high with back issues of *The Gazette* to see anything else.

"Mr. Teller?" she asked timidly.

"That's me," the man said, pushing his glasses onto the top of his head. He was mostly bald, with a craggy face and very bushy eyebrows that made him look a little frightening. "And you must be the girl who called about the horses—Lisa, is it?" He smiled at her. He had one of the nicest smiles Lisa had ever seen. As soon as he smiled, she wasn't frightened any more.

"Lisa Atwood," she said, sighing with relief.

"Come sit down," Mr. Teller said. He glanced around. "There must be a chair here someplace. This office is famous for its walking piles of papers, you know. If I turn my back on a clear space, some pile of papers comes to fill it up!"

Lisa laughed. He stood up and moved some papers off a chair onto the floor. Lisa sat down quickly. She turned to the pile he'd just made on the floor. "Sit, and stay!" she commanded.

Mr. Teller laughed at her joke. "I think we're going to get along," he said. Lisa knew he was right. "Now, tell me again about this idea of yours."

"It's about horses," she began. "See, I ride at Pine Hollow. A lot of other girls and some boys in town do, too. It's a very busy place. There are lessons and classes, horses being born and trained. There are shows and events. Not everybody is interested, of course, but there's so much going on there that's *news* for the young riders in town that I think you should have a column about it in the paper."

"Interesting," Mr. Teller said, sitting back in his chair. "Any idea who might be able to cover the subject?"

Lisa knew he was teasing her a bit. He already knew that she wanted to write it because she'd told him on the telephone.

Lisa blushed. "Well, I have a lot of experience writing," she said. "I do well on my papers in school—I've brought you a few samples . . ." She reached for her portfolio.

"It's okay," Mr. Teller said. "I believe you get good grades, but how well you write classroom essays may not have anything to do with how well you write newspaper columns."

"I thought you might say that," Lisa told him. "That's why I also brought you some samples of the writing I did for the school newspaper last year." She handed him three of her favorite stories. One was about a new science teacher. The other two covered her class field trips.

"Good thinking," he said. He glanced quickly at the clippings. "Hmmm . . ." He looked up at her. "Okay, Lisa, you can write. What's the angle here?"

This was the moment Lisa had dreamed about all

last night—when she'd been sleeping. She'd actually spent most of the night awake, worrying about this interview. In her imagination, it had *never* gone as smoothly as this. "'Hoof Beat,'" she said, looking Mr. Teller straight in the eye. "The name of the column is Hoof Beat." Lisa thought that was pretty clever. Since the subject a reporter covered was called a beat, and since she'd be covering horses, Hoof Beat seemed the perfect choice.

Mr. Teller leaned back in his chair again. Lisa had the feeling he always did that when he was thinking. He looked to the left and to the right, though there was nothing in either direction for him to see but piles of papers. Finally, he looked at Lisa again.

"Deal," he said. "I want five hundred to seven hundred and fifty words a week. That's two to three typed pages. Copy is due Wednesday noon. It's your byline, I won't make changes in the stories, unless I have to correct English. You can come in Tuesday night and use the typewriter over there if you want."

Lisa looked dubiously at the ancient relic. "No thanks. We've got a computer at home. I'll use that. It's easier for me."

"Would be for me, too," Mr. Teller joked. "Anyway, I'll pay you fifteen dollars a column."

"You'll *pay* me?" Lisa couldn't believe she'd heard the words correctly. She was stunned. "Every week?"

"Of course I'll pay you," Mr. Teller said gruffly. "If I don't pay you, you may start thinking this isn't important. It *is* important. I'm going to be counting on two to three pages of copy from you every week. I'll hold space for it. If you let me down, I'll be in trouble. I don't want that. You don't want to not get paid. See?"

Lisa just nodded. She was too excited to speak.

"All right. This is Thursday. Think you can have your first column in by next Wednesday?"

For fifteen dollars, she'd have it in that afternoon! "Yes, sir, Chief!" she said, standing at attention. Her portfolio fell onto the floor and her A papers were scattered everywhere. She flushed with embarrassment.

"See what I mean about paper walking around this office?" Mr. Teller said, crouching to help her pick up the mess. Lisa smiled, knowing he was trying to make her feel better. "Oh, and one more thing . . ."

"Yes?"

"Don't call me Chief. 'Mr. Teller' will do nicely."

Lisa stuffed the last of the papers into her portfolio, shook her new boss's hand, called him Mr. Teller, not Chief, and left the office.

Lisa practically floated down the stairs, she was so excited. She was a reporter—with a beat of her own! This was the most exciting thing that had happened to her since she'd discovered horseback riding. She had a job. It was a real job, the start of a real career.

Sure, she told herself, *The Willow Creek Gazette* wasn't exactly *The Washington Post* or *The New York Times*, but it was a start. After all, she was only thirteen. If she got a running start at her age, she could land something bigger on the *Post* while she was in college. Maybe get bylines. Investigative reporting was what she'd aim for. She could go undercover, tracking mobsters and drug smugglers or maybe even uncover government scandals. She'd go to war zones and interview soldiers, talk to dictators and presidents. And spy stories—she could reveal double agents who were jeopardizing democracy. With that kind of reporting, she'd get a Pulitzer Prize—maybe two! And that would bring her to the attention of the Nobel Committee . . .

But first, she realized with a start, she had to write an article about training Samson.

3

STEVIE STILL COULDN'T believe how cute Samson was. She'd seen him being born and she'd watched him stand and nurse for the first time. Since then, she'd seen him almost every day—and each time she saw him it was as exciting as the first time.

He was a lot bigger, of course. He'd grown a tremendous amount in the first months of his life, but he was still little and he was still very cute.

Samson stayed near his mother most of the time, though now he would sometimes venture as far away as the other side of the paddock, a distance of perhaps twenty feet. But if somebody approached the paddock, Samson would usually trot quickly to his mother's side. Delilah was always there waiting for him. She'd nuzzle him and comfort him when he was frightened. Stevie thought she was a very good and attentive mother.

Stevie was alone with Samson and Delilah today. Carole, she knew, was at the shopping center, volunteering for the library. Lisa had promised to come help Stevie later. She'd called Stevie in the morning, saying something about an appointment. She had been awfully vague. Normally, this would have upset Stevie, partly because of her curiosity and partly because she had been counting on Lisa's help. However, she was excited about being the only person working with Samson. She'd watched Carole the day before and was sure she could do it. It would be a lot of fun, too.

"Hi, there," she said, greeting mother and son in their paddock. Delilah glanced at her with little interest. Samson snuggled up to his mother's side.

The first thing Stevie did was to put a halter on Delilah, then she fastened the lead rope to the fence of the paddock. Delilah cooperated the way she always did. There was no problem at all.

"Good girl," Stevie said, patting her firmly on the neck. She wanted to show Samson that she was friends with his mother. "See, boy, you can trust me. Your mom and I are old pals."

The foal ducked around his mother's rear.

"I mean it," Stevie said to him. "We've ridden together lots. She'll tell you. As a matter of fact, she even tried to throw me once, but I held on!"

That was a vivid memory to Stevie. The first year she'd been a rider, she'd ridden Delilah on a trail. She had been wearing sneakers and her foot had slipped out of the stirrup and the stirrup had started banging on Delilah's belly. Not surprisingly, the horse hadn't liked that at all and had started acting up. Stevie had held on to her mane for dear life, and most important, she'd gotten her footing again. It had been enough to make her want to wear cowboy-style boots with a high heel now when she rode.

"Good old pals," Stevie repeated. Then she climbed up over the fence and into the paddock. She walked along Delilah's side, approaching Samson slowly. She didn't want to frighten him. She held the halter in her left hand, behind her back. She showed him her empty right hand. He didn't seem very interested in it. He stepped back, away from her.

Stevie stepped toward him. He stepped back again. She tried again. He did it again.

"This is almost like dancing class!" she said.

She moved to the right. He moved to the left. She shifted. So did he. She giggled.

Stevie hopped a few inches off the ground. Samson fled, running all the way around the ring until he came to the far side of his mother. Then he snuggled up to her.

Stevie crept around Delilah's rear. Softly, she put her hand on Samson's flank. He moved away from her again.

She loved to watch him move. There was something about the colt's gaits that was different from an adult horse's gaits. Stevie realized that it must have to do with the proportions of the animal. The colt's legs were relatively longer than his mother's, and he almost seemed to bounce as he moved. Stevie could have watched him for hours.

Samson took cover next to his mother. Stevie peered under Delilah's belly at the colt.

"Peekaboo!" she said, startling the colt. He bolted, quickly circling the paddock. He returned to his mother, staying on the side away from Stevie. Once again, she peered under Delilah's belly. This time, Samson was waiting for her. He peered right back at her. "Peekaboo!" she said, and he circled the paddock.

"Smart boy!" Stevie said, genuinely impressed that the colt had learned the game so quickly. Playing with Samson was as much fun as playing with a puppy, and Stevie quickly found that he liked fun and games.

Stevie slung Samson's halter over the edge of the paddock fence and the lead rope with it. It was going to be easier playing games without being bothered by those things.

Stevie tried several varieties of peekaboo—sometimes meeting up with Samson under his mother, sometimes in front, and sometimes behind. Delilah stood obediently still, ignoring the shenanigans of her colt and Stevie. Stevie wasn't surprised that Delilah didn't participate in any way. She was a well-trained horse and knew that when she'd been haltered and tied someplace, it was her job to stand still and await further instructions.

When Stevie tired of peekaboo, she taught Samson how to play tag. Samson won hands down. Every time Stevie reached for him, he dodged her and ran in the opposite direction. He was good—really good. She tried faking him out, reaching first with her right hand, and then when he began moving away from her reach, she'd quickly extend her left hand and tap him with that. It only took Samson a bit to figure out that the surefire way to evade her was to back up and turn around. And when Stevie chased after him, he just ran faster.

Stevie was beginning to wonder if she could teach Samson to play follow-the-leader when Lisa arrived.

"Come on in and see what I've taught Samson!" Stevie said, inviting Lisa to join the fun.

"I think I'd rather watch," Lisa said. "Unless you need me, I mean."

"No, we're having a ball. I never knew a horse as smart as this! Wait'll you see."

Stevie demonstrated peekaboo and tag. Lisa could hardly believe what she was watching. She'd seen horses trained to do some very complicated things, but she'd never seen a horse having as much fun as this.

"You try," Stevie said. "I'm sure you'll be as good at it as I am. He makes it easy."

Lisa was tempted. It looked like an awful lot of fun. But she had a job to do. She had a column to write and she wanted to surprise her friends with it. Now she really had something to write about!

"I can't," Lisa said to Stevie. "There's something I have to do."

"But you just *got* here," Stevie reminded her.

"I know, but . . . well, I've got to do it."

Stevie could tell there was something Lisa was keeping from her, but right then she was having too much fun with Samson to care what Lisa was up to. She just told Lisa she'd talk to her later and returned to her games, barely noticing as Lisa left for home.

Follow-the-leader, it turned out, was a much harder game to play. She walked ahead of Samson and then skipped, sort of like a trot. He was following her all right, but she didn't think he was doing what she'd been doing. The only way she could tell was if she stopped and turned around. Every time she stopped and turned around, she found that Samson had stopped, too, and was looking straight at her. Then, if she tried to let *him* be the leader, all he did was to go over and stand by Delilah. The third time he did it, he also began nuzzling his mother for something to eat.

Stevie realized that she, too, was beginning to be hungry, and since she was also rather tired, Samson was probably tired as well. She glanced at her watch. It was nearly one o'clock. She'd been playing with Samson for more than two hours—and it seemed as if it had been just a few minutes. She'd only promised Carole to be with the colt for fifteen or twenty minutes, but that had turned out to be not nearly enough. Wouldn't Carole be pleased!

She didn't want to disturb the nursing colt. He seemed so peaceful, in sharp contrast to the lively little creature she'd just been playing with. Stevie climbed up on the paddock fence, loosened Delilah's lead rope, removed her halter, and then climbed down. She was halfway back to the tack room before she remembered the halter and lead rope she'd brought out for Samson, which she'd never had the chance to use. She returned to the paddock and found the contented little colt lying down on the cool earth in a shady spot of the paddock, sleeping very soundly. She grabbed the halter and lead and took them back into the stable.

She was greeted by the familiar and unpleasant smell of fresh paint. "Ick," she said, wrinkling her nose. There was nobody around to sympathize with her. Most of the girls who were usually in her class were on the trail with Red O'Malley. Stevie could have gone with them, but she'd had a lot more fun with Samson.

She was about to sit on the bench nearest her cubby when she realized the bench was sparkling white and obviously freshly painted. Her jeans certainly didn't need a white stripe across the seat!

Complaining out loud to nobody, she sat down on the floor and pulled her backpack out of her cubby. She'd wear her jeans home, but she wanted to switch into her sneakers first. Boots were great for riding, or working in the paddock, but not for walking.

It only took a few seconds to make the change. She

didn't even bother tying her laces. She rammed her boots back into her cubby, zipped up her backpack, and was ready to go when she realized that she hadn't seen her wallet—not that it mattered much. She'd spent three of her four cents on a chewy mint and that didn't leave much in the way of spending money. Still, she didn't want to lose the wallet. It had her library card in it.

She checked her backpack. It wasn't there, not even in the outside zipper compartment. Annoyed, she sat back down on the floor and pulled her boots out of her cubby, figuring that she must have shoved it into the back when she put her boots away. It wasn't there.

Stevie was annoyed with herself. She didn't like to lose things. She knew she hadn't taken it out of her backpack since she put it there the day before, but it looked as if it was gone. Not that it was a valuable wallet; nor that she had much money in it, certainly nothing to steal. It was just that . . . Then she remembered: Carole's money had been in the wallet. Carole had asked her to hold on to her fifteen dollars so she could buy her father a birthday present—and it looked a lot like it had been stolen!

Stevie suddenly had an awful empty feeling in the pit of her stomach. Fifteen dollars! How could this have happened?

The cubbies weren't locked, but everybody at the stable knew everybody, and it was hard to imagine who would steal something from a friend. Certainly Carole didn't take it. Lisa was out of the question, too.

Stevie's vivid imagination went to work. First, she tried to remember who had been there when Carole had given her the money, but it just didn't seem possible that one of the other young riders could have taken the wallet. One of the stableboys? she asked herself. She shook her head. Perhaps it was an outside job— maybe someone wandered in off the street, into the empty locker area, just looking for loose wallets. That at least seemed possible, but it was a little difficult to imagine thieves who would waste their time in the kids' locker area of a stable. Stevie realized she was about to daydream up an international plot, so she stopped herself. At that moment it didn't matter how the wallet had disappeared. It did matter that it *had* disappeared. She needed to talk to Max.

Stevie found Max in Barq's stall, examining a hoof. He angled the horse's hoof so that it was centered in the stream of sunlight slanting across the stall. He alternated cleaning out the hoof with a hoof-pick and gently prodding the hoof tissues with his fingers. Stevie waited. She wasn't feeling patient, but it would be useless to try to interrupt Max while he was caring for a horse.

"Got it!" he announced finally. He eased the hoof-pick between the horse's shoe and foot and manipulated it gently until a pebble dropped into the straw on the floor of the stall. Max released Barq's hoof. The horse put it back onto the ground and continued munching at his hay as if nothing had happened.

"What's up, Stevie?" Max asked as he stepped out of the stall and fastened the door behind him. "I saw you heading for Samson's paddock; everything okay there?"

"Oh, sure, Samson and I had a great workout," she said. "But I do have a problem." She told him about her wallet and Carole's money.

"Boy, that's tough," he said. He shook his head sadly, sympathetically.

"Sure is," she said, sensing that Max would find a way to solve the problem. "I knew you'd help me out."

"Oh, I'm not sure there's anything I can really do to help, Stevie," Max said. "But you've learned something."

This was definitely *not* what Stevie was hoping he would say. He was saying exactly what her parents would say.

"That's not fair, Max," Stevie wailed. "The money got stolen. In *your* stables. I couldn't help it."

"Stevie, this is a public place. There are no locks on the cubbies. They are there for the convenience of our riders—not for security. I'm sorry about Carole's money, but it was careless of you to stash that much money in an open area. Next time, just remember that I can lock valuables in my desk."

He walked toward his office. Stevie trailed after him. She just had to get him to help her.

"Next time? There won't be a next time, Max! Carole will never speak to me again! It's money for her dad's birthday! Do something!"

"Maybe I should," he said thoughtfully.

Stevie waited. The fact that it was Carole's money had swayed him, she was sure. Max scratched his head thoughtfully.

"I know," he continued. "As soon as we finish with the paint job, I'll put another sign up in the locker room about locking valuables in the office."

A lot of good that'll do me, Stevie thought. Angry and disgusted, she went home.

4

THAT EVENING, LISA sat on the comfortable chair in her room, her legs over one of the soft arms, her back against the other. She was thinking.

She'd already made a list of things she could write about in her first column. That was good. The problem was that there were more than fifteen items on the list and there was no way she could write about fifteen things in five hundred words. Mostly she wanted to write about Samson's training, but there was so much to describe about it that she hardly knew where to begin. She needed an angle. Then she got an idea.

The New Student, she wrote.

> *Pine Hollow Stables' newest student is also its youngest. His name is Samson. He's two months old.*

*He's about four feet tall, has short black hair, pointed
ears, and a cute tail. He is Delilah's colt.*

Lisa liked it. She thought it was a good idea to make
the point that it wasn't just the riders who learned at
the stable. The horses had to learn, too.

Lisa was about to describe the colt's first lessons when
her mother called upstairs to tell her the phone was for
her. She'd been so interested in what she was writing
that she hadn't even heard the phone ring. She
reached across to her bedside table and picked up the
receiver.

"Oh, Lisa, I'm so glad you're there!" Stevie said.
Lisa recognized the frantic tone in Stevie's voice im-
mediately. It didn't concern her too much, though.
Stevie often had a frantic tone.

"What's up?" Lisa asked, still gazing proudly at the
paragraph she'd written.

"It's Carole's money—it's gone!" Stevie said.

Then Lisa knew Stevie had a good reason for the
frantic tone.

Stevie told her what had happened. "It just wasn't
there when I came back from the training session. Did
you see anybody lurking near the cubbies when you
were there?"

Lisa thought for a minute. "The place stank so
much from the paint job that I just ran through," she
said. "I didn't see anybody, but that doesn't mean anything. They could have been there."

"I know they could. They *were*. And you know, I've been thinking. Remember the time Polly Giacomin couldn't find her riding crop?"

Lisa did remember. Polly had been so upset about it, she'd cried all through their class. "What a baby she was!" Lisa said.

"Maybe, but it never did show up. And remember when Meg couldn't find her keys?"

"Sure, but who would take her keys?"

"I don't know, but I'll bet you *anything* it was the same person who took my wallet."

"You think there's somebody stealing stuff from the cubbies?" Lisa asked, now very interested.

"Let's just say that I think it looks suspicious," Stevie said.

Suspicious was just the word. And when there was something suspicious going on, people needed to know about it. Lisa tore a piece of paper from her pad and picked up her pen again.

Suspicious Thefts at Pine Hollow! she wrote.

On the other end of the line, sitting in the Lakes' kitchen, telephone at her ear, Stevie waited for Lisa to offer to lend her money. But Lisa was quiet. "So, listen," Stevie said. "Can you help me out?"

"You bet I can!" Lisa said.

The words she'd been waiting to hear. "All fifteen dollars?" Stevie asked.

"Oh, no. Not that way," Lisa said. "Sorry. I'm broke now. But I'll help you another way."

"You sound just like Max," Stevie said grumpily.

"Huh?" Lisa responded.

"I suppose *you* think it's my fault, too," Stevie said.

Lisa didn't answer. Stevie thought she'd sounded kind of distracted. She was about to give her a piece of her mind when there was an interruption. Her mother entered the kitchen and with her was the most amazing girl Stevie had ever seen.

"Stevie, this is Trudy," Mrs. Lake said. "Trudy, this is my daughter, Stephanie."

"Lisa, I've got to go," Stevie said, hanging up the phone hastily, all thoughts of Carole's fifteen dollars fleeing from her mind.

She spun on the kitchen stool to face Trudy and then blinked her eyes to be sure it was for real. Trudy was a girl about her own age, and that was where the resemblance between them stopped, for Trudy was dressed in the most outlandish outfit Stevie had ever seen.

First of all, she was wearing an oversize Hawaiian-pattern shirt, over a black spandex skirt. She wore purple tights blotched with yellow splatters, with black bobby socks over the tights, and black gym shoes. On each wrist there were at least ten plastic hoop bracelets of bright colors to match her shirt. Her earrings were big yellow plastic hoops. She wore eye shadow that picked up a lot of the colors from her Hawaiian shirt and the bracelets. And then there was her hair. Her hair was bleached blond and cut straight. On her right side, it was cut above her ear. It got longer and longer as the hairstyle continued around her head, until on her left side it hung below her chin line. She wore a bow smack on top of her head, made of the same material as her Hawaiian shirt.

Stevie decided she looked wonderful. "Is it Halloween already?" Stevie asked with a grin.

"You like it?" Trudy responded.

"I've never seen anything like it," Stevie told her. "Even when we were in New York, where there were some pretty wild looks, nobody dressed like that!"

"I put the outfit together myself," Trudy said.

Stevie slid off the stool, picked up one of Trudy's suitcases, and said, "Come on, I'll show you to our room. We're sharing. Hope that's okay."

"Sure," Trudy said. She picked up the other bag and followed Stevie up the stairs.

Stevie dropped Trudy's suitcase in the corner of her room. Trudy piled the one she was carrying on top.

"That's your bed," Stevie said, pointing and sitting down on her own bed. Trudy sat on hers. "Does your mother actually *let* you dress like that?" Stevie asked enviously.

"Not really," Trudy said, smiling mischievously. "I mean, she wouldn't exactly choose these clothes for me, but see, I'm on a clothing allowance, so I get to buy what I want. And this is what I want."

"Cool," Stevie said. "But how do you do the eye makeup?"

34

Trudy offered to show her. Within ten minutes, the bathroom was littered with little plastic containers and foam-rubber applicators. The two girls stood side by side, stretching to be close to the mirror. Trudy demonstrated how to mix colors for the most interesting effect.

"I'm getting this funny feeling," Stevie said, admiring the pink and blue butterfly she'd just drawn over her right eye.

"What's that?" Trudy asked.

"I have a suspicion that our mothers thought that if you and I got together for a couple of weeks, I might be a good influence on you."

Trudy exploded into a fit of giggles. "We'll show them," she said.

"Yeah, but that's not even the funniest part," Stevie said. "The funniest part is that I think it's the first time in my life anybody's ever thought I would be a good influence on anybody! Hey, what do you think about a little silver lining on the lower wing of the butterfly?"

"I think gold would be better," Trudy told her. "It'll match the sparkles we're about to put on your cheeks!"

"*Outrageous!*"

LATER THAT NIGHT, Stevie lay back in bed, watching the patterns that car headlights made on the ceiling of her room. Trudy slept soundly in the bed next to hers. It had been such a busy day that she really needed some time to think about everything that had happened. At first, all she could think of were the wonderful things that had happened, training Samson and meeting Trudy. Then she recalled the bad news about Trudy. She didn't ride horses. She'd never ridden horses, and she wasn't especially enthusiastic about learning to ride horses. Stevie would change that, she was sure.

Then there was the matter of Carole's money. Nothing was going right on that. Max wouldn't make it up to her. Lisa wouldn't give it to her. She just had to get fifteen dollars for Carole. There was no way she could earn it in time. She was going to be much too busy having fun with Samson and Trudy to take on any old baby-sitting jobs. Besides, she'd tried to earn money in the past and hadn't been awfully successful at it. And she certainly couldn't *steal* it like the jerk who had taken Carole's money in the first place. That left only one possibility. She would have to borrow it. From whom?

Her mother? No way. Once her mother learned how it had gotten lost, she wouldn't lend her any money. She'd say exactly what Max had said. Her father? Ditto. Her brothers? Now there was a possibility. She knew that her twin brother, Alex, still had some of his birthday money left. He might lend it to her—but he would want interest. Maybe Michael, her little brother, could be talked into a loan. Her oldest brother, Chad, was out of the question. She didn't call him Scrooge for nothing! She decided to approach Alex and Michael first thing in the morning.

There was something else she had to do first thing in the morning. She had to begin working on Trudy to get her to ride. Trudy was a really neat person, but it would be hard for her to be a close friend unless she could ride. The image of Trudy on horseback made Stevie smile to herself in the dark of her room. She just hoped that horses were color-blind!

THERE WERE TIMES, Lisa thought, when Stevie was just too much. This was one of them.

It was the day after the disappearance of Stevie's wallet and the appearance of Trudy. Their riding class was over and The Saddle Club was about to give Samson his next lesson. Stevie was in the locker area of the stable where their classmates were changing out of their riding clothes. Stevie was telling absolutely everybody about the theft of Carole's money, asking them if they could lend her some, and telling them not to tell Carole. Lisa was quite certain that a secret shared by fifteen girls would not be a secret for long!

And to top it off, Stevie had talked Trudy into keeping Carole away.

"Don't let her out of your sight," Stevie had said. "Stick to her like a tattoo."

38

Lisa thought that it was an appropriate phrase. Trudy, after all, was dressed like a tattoo! In any event, Trudy and Carole were well out of earshot and Stevie was doing her sales pitch.

"It's money she's been saving for months for her father's birthday!" Stevie told Anna McWhirter, one of the girls. "It was stolen in broad daylight!"

"I don't have a penny to spare," Anna told Stevie. "I'm saving up to buy myself a new riding hat."

"What happened to the old one?" Stevie asked.

"It just disappeared one day. It was getting too small for me anyway. But until I buy a new one, I have to use the ones here and I'd rather have my own."

Just disappeared? That seemed very mysterious to Lisa, and strangely consistent with some other things she'd been observing recently.

"It seems like things are always disappearing around here," Veronica diAngelo said. "I've never found the riding gloves I used for the gymkhana. They were *very* expensive, too. I know somebody stole them."

Usually, Lisa instantly dismissed everything snooty Veronica said. In this case, she thought she might make an exception.

Stevie spun to look at Veronica. Lisa knew just what was on her mind. Veronica was very rich. She was the daughter of one of the wealthiest men in town. She was also an unbearable snob and The Saddle Club girls despised her. Nevertheless, in Stevie's current state of panic, all Stevie was going to be thinking of was how rich Veronica was. Lisa knew Stevie was going to ask Veronica to lend her the fifteen dollars. Lisa knew she wouldn't be able to watch Stevie with a straight face, so she left the locker area. Stevie gave her a dirty look.

Lisa headed through the stable and across to Samson's paddock.

Trudy stood next to the fence, outside the paddock. She watched Carole silently.

"Isn't he cute?" Lisa asked.

"Yeah," Trudy said. "Nice pony."

"He's actually not a pony," Lisa said. "A pony is a *small* horse, not a young horse. Samson is a foal or a colt. When he grows up, he'll be a horse." Lisa liked explaining horse facts to other people. It didn't seem like it was so long ago that she didn't know anything— when she would have made a mistake like that. She was proud of all she'd learned. It was going to be fun to have somebody new to teach about horses.

"Looks like a pony to me," Trudy said.

Lisa decided to hold off on the lessons for a bit. It was just possible that Trudy wasn't as eager a student as Lisa had been.

Carole finished putting the halter and lead rope on Delilah. She handed the lead to Lisa, who looped it around the cleat on the outside of the ring. Lisa knew that the cleat was on the outside for the horses' safety, and she was all ready to explain it to Trudy, but Trudy didn't seem very interested. Lisa just did the small chore and returned to Trudy's side.

Once again, Carole patted Delilah's neck to show Samson that they were friends. She held the colt's halter and lead in her other hand behind her back. Carole was aware that Samson was watching her alertly. As before, she approached him calmly, expecting him to stay by his mother's side where she could put the halter on him.

It didn't go that way. As soon as she rounded Delilah's rear, Samson took off. That was odd. He didn't seem frightened of her, he just seemed to want to run. Since she'd rarely seen him run before, except when his mother was also running, she was surprised. She stood still next to Delilah. Samson returned, taking shelter on Delilah's other side.

Carole peered around Delilah's rear. Samson peered around Delilah's rear. Carole spotted Samson. Samson spotted Carole and hid again quickly. Carole smiled to herself. It was just as if he were playing peekaboo. She squatted down to look at the colt from under his mother's belly. Samson lowered his head and looked through Delilah's legs at Carole. As soon as he could see her, he withdrew. Carole laughed again. He *was* playing peekaboo.

It was fun, but it wasn't training.

Carole stood up and walked calmly around Delilah's rear. She paused for just a second, but it was enough. Samson took off like a shot. He circled the paddock and then returned to his mother's other side. Carole tried again. So did Samson.

"What's going on with you?" she asked. His answer was to run away again.

It didn't seem as if he was frightened. He didn't run in fear. Instead, it was more as if he were playing a game—just the way he'd played peekaboo, only this time, it was tag and she was It.

When Samson went to circle the paddock yet another time, Carole decided to show him she wasn't playing the game. She left Delilah's side and walked over to Trudy and Lisa.

"What's going on with him?" Carole asked.

"I wonder if you could teach him to fetch," Trudy said. "I got my dog to do it very easily. That kind of game seems to come naturally to a lot of animals."

Carole ignored the suggestion. The purpose was not to teach Samson games, but to teach him to wear a halter.

"Was he doing this yesterday?" Carole asked Lisa.

"Oh, yes," Lisa said. "Stevie had a great time with him."

"Did she get the halter on him?" Carole asked.

"I don't know," Lisa answered. "I couldn't stay very long. But I know she spent a lot of time with him, so she must have." Lisa glanced at her watch. "Oops, I've got to get going now. See you!"

Carole noticed that there was something secretive about Lisa, and she seemed to be doing a lot of disappearing lately. Normally, Carole would have been very

curious. Today, however, she was much more interested in what was going on with Samson.

"Okay, see you," she said. She returned her attention to Samson. "Come on, boy. It's time for you to
learn some manners."

If Samson thought that the proper way to respond to
somebody who was walking toward him was to run,
then she'd just have to teach him to walk toward somebody who was standing still. He had to learn to come
to a call.

She stood next to Delilah and whistled. Samson's
ears perked up. He looked at her, interested. She whistled again. She continued that until, finally, the colt
walked over to her. As soon as he was within an arm's
length of her, she reached out to pat him—his reward.
It was the signal he'd been waiting for, so he bolted,
playing tag again.

Trudy laughed. Carole did not.

"It's so *funny!*" Trudy said.

"Not from where I'm standing," Carole said. She
tried again. The same thing happened several times
until, finally, the horse realized that Carole wasn't
playing the same game he was. He stood still long
enough for her to pat him, but it was nowhere near
long enough for her to put the halter on him.

"It's as if we've never done this before," she said in
total frustration. "Somehow, he's forgotten everything
I taught him just two days ago. Poor Stevie must have

had a terrible time yesterday. Did she say anything to you?"

"Not at all," Trudy said. "She just said she had a lot of fun."

"Well, this isn't fun. He must not have been doing this!"

Carole held out the halter for Samson to examine. He looked at it very tentatively, curiously. She remained still, not wanting to distract the excitable colt. He stepped toward her extended hand.

"I don't believe that girl!" Stevie huffed, storming out of the stable area. "Veronica diAngelo is just impossible. Impossible. She wouldn't give me the time of day, much less lend me money. I must have been crazy to ask her!"

Samson bolted.

Carole sighed. Nothing was going right today. Just when there seemed to be a chance that Samson might learn something, she was interrupted. There was no point in losing her temper at Stevie, though. That was just the way she was.

"What's the problem?" Carole asked resignedly.

"All I did was ask Veronica a simple question—"

"Nothing about Veronica is ever simple," Carole reminded her. "So what did you ask?"

"I've just got to get some money," Stevie said. "So I thought maybe she could lend me some. You wouldn't be able to lend me a few dollars, would you?"

"Stevie, you know I'm saving up every penny for my dad's birthday."

Carole could have sworn that Stevie blushed. "Oh, yeah, right," Stevie said. "Well, I'm not all that desperate, so forget I even mentioned it, will you?"

Stevie grabbed Trudy's arm and pulled her back toward the stable.

Carole reflected on her day so far and quickly concluded that *everybody* was acting strangely. Lisa was into a disappearing act; if Stevie was desperate enough to try to borrow money from Veronica, she was in trouble; Samson wasn't doing any of the things she'd worked so hard to train him to do the other day. And Trudy? Carole suspected that Trudy wasn't any more strange that day than she usually was, but that was strange enough!

It was time to quit for the day. Carole climbed up over the fence, took off Delilah's halter and lead rope, and returned the tack to the tack room.

Some days, nothing went right.

LISA COULDN'T HELP grinning. She opened the copy of *The Willow Creek Gazette* and read the words "Hoof Beat by Lisa Atwood."

It was like a dream come true. The article had come out to just six hundred words and Mr. Teller had seemed happy about that. Most of the article just listed the classes Max offered for young riders. Mr. Teller had said she had to include that even though it didn't really seem like news. The last part *was* news.

> And there's bad news at Pine Hollow this week: Stevie Lake's wallet was stolen out of her cubby while she was working in the stable. The wallet had more than $15 cash in it.
>
> There were apparently no other young riders at the stable at the time of the theft, but many of the riders

knew that Stevie would be there at that time and that she had the cash in her wallet. Stevie was holding the money for her friend Carole Hanson, who had worked and saved the money to buy her father a birthday present. This reporter hopes that whoever took the money will come forward and return it. If it is returned right away, nothing will be said.

Lisa sighed happily. She was glad both that she had news to report and that she'd done it in such a good way. She'd told what had happened, but even more important, she'd given somebody the opportunity to correct the wrong that had been done. Maybe the thief thought she could get away with it. Or maybe, just maybe, the thief was beginning to feel bad, and with the encouragement from her article would have second thoughts about taking somebody else's property and return it.

Carefully, Lisa folded the newspaper and put it in her backpack to take to the stable. Most people in town did read the paper, and it was probable that they would have noticed *The Gazette*'s newest feature, but just in case, she wanted to have it with her.

It seemed to Lisa that the fifteen-minute walk to Pine Hollow had never gone faster. The whole way there, she thought about how pleased Stevie was going to be with what she'd done—how she'd asked the thief to return the money. And she also thought about how relieved Carole would be to have the story out in the open so that she had a real shot at getting her money back. Most of all, she thought about how jealous absolutely everybody was going to be. She, Lisa Atwood, had her own column in *The Gazette*.

She was still floating on air when she entered the locker area. The whole place was full of her classmates. They were all talking to one another in little groups. In one corner, Polly Giacomin was showing some friends a new pair of sandals. In another, Betsy Cavanaugh was talking furiously with two other girls. Anna McWhirter was talking with Lorraine Olson. Lisa was thrilled. Almost certainly, everybody was talking about her.

The first person who spotted her was Stevie. She and Trudy had been standing near the doorway, talking intensely.

"Did you see?" Lisa asked proudly, pulling the paper out of her backpack.

She was expecting Stevie to shriek with joy. Stevie shrieked all right, but it wasn't with joy.

"How could you do that to me!" she shrieked.

"What do you mean?"

"Writing about losing Carole's money—she's furious at me now! I'd already borrowed six dollars to give to her. I was going to get the rest in time, but you blew it. She may never speak to me again!"

Lisa was genuinely surprised to learn that Stevie hadn't even told Carole about it yet. Carole was her best friend. How could Lisa have known Stevie would keep something like that from Carole?

"But you'd *have* to tell her eventually," Lisa said. "I just saved you the trouble."

"Maybe I *would* have had to tell her eventually," Stevie said, "but *I* should have done it, not you." She spun on her heel and returned to the bench next to her cubby.

That sounded exactly right to Lisa. Stevie *should* have done it. Stevie was angry at her for doing something she should have done in the first place! It was just like Stevie to lose her temper without thinking over what she was saying, Lisa thought. She'd get over it. In the meantime, she wasn't going to let Stevie's little temper tantrum interfere with her pleasure over her first publication.

She ignored Stevie and found an empty cubby next to where Anna McWhirter was sitting. "Did you see?" Lisa asked, brandishing *The Gazette.*

"I saw," Anna said coldly. Lisa suspected she was jealous. She'd get over that in time. Jealousy would eventually turn to admiration, she was sure.

"Do you think it'll make the thief return the wallet?" Lisa asked.

"It wasn't me, so you can just forget about that!" Anna said. She gave her boot a final tug, stood up, and walked away.

That surprised Lisa. She hadn't expected that kind

of reaction at all. Then she remembered that Anna's hat had been stolen, too. Lisa decided that Anna was jealous all right. She was jealous that Lisa had mentioned the theft of the wallet, but not of Anna's hat. Well, she could do something about that in the next article she wrote, but it would be a week until that one came out.

Lisa busied herself getting ready for class, but her mind was on her next article. She didn't notice when Veronica diAngelo came and stood next to her.

"I suppose you brought a search warrant," Veronica said. "You can look all you want in my cubby for Stevie's wallet. You won't find it there."

Veronica spun around and walked away too fast for Lisa to respond—but she wouldn't have been able to say anything anyway. Lisa was more than a little surprised by Veronica's reaction. Veronica was always convinced that everything she did was better than anything anybody else ever did. She was the last person at the stable that Lisa would have expected to be jealous. It made Lisa feel good that Veronica was so obviously jealous of *her*. Maybe, like Anna, she was a little jealous of Carole, too, just because Lisa hadn't said anything about the theft of Veronica's riding gloves.

Lisa finished pulling on her boots, collected the tack for Pepper, the horse she usually rode in class, and was about to leave the locker area when she noticed a tight knot of girls in one corner. Betsy Cavanaugh was in the center, her face red with anger and streaked with tears. Lisa had always liked Betsy. She didn't like to see her so upset about something.

"What's the matter with Betsy?" she asked, walking over to the group.

"It's none of your business," Meg Durham spat out angrily.

"Oh, yes, it is," Betsy said, overriding Meg. Then she turned to Lisa. "Look," she said. "Just because I was here when Carole gave Stevie the money doesn't mean I took it."

"I never said you did," Lisa told her.

"Well, you said one of us took it and there weren't all that many of us there at the time. Two people have already asked me about it, but I'm telling you, I didn't take it! If you want to know who did, why don't you find out who just bought herself a new pair of sandals!"

Betsy glared at Lisa, ignoring the tears as they spilled out of her eyes and down her cheeks. Lisa was really sorry Betsy was so upset. Lisa doubted that Betsy had anything to do with the theft because she was such a nice girl. Sometimes the truth hurt, she realized. And sometimes the people who got hurt by the truth were innocent people, like Betsy.

Betsy wiped her tears with her bare hand, streaking her face even more. Lisa always carried tissues. It was one of the things her mother made her do. She pulled the little tissue pack out of her pocket and offered it to Betsy.

"No thank you," Betsy said. "I've gotten enough

from you already today." She sniffed and then turned her back on Lisa. Confused, Lisa shook her head and walked away. It was time to tack up Pepper.

Pepper, it seemed, was the only one who wasn't jealous or angry at her, she mused as she slipped his bridle over his head.

"Oh, you're here," Carole said, genuine surprise apparent in her voice.

Lisa looked up, startled; she hadn't heard anyone's footsteps. "Of course I'm here, where else did you think I would be ten minutes before class?" Lisa asked. An awful lot of people seemed to be behaving very strangely today. She had the sinking feeling Carole was going to be another one of them.

"Hiding out," Carole said. "But you're brave."

Lisa finished buckling the bridle and turned her attention to Pepper's saddle. "I heard you're not speaking to Stevie. Why? Because she lost your money?"

"No. Because she didn't tell me about it."

"I told her she should have," Lisa said, feeling vindicated.

"You told *everyone* she should have," Carole said.

Then Lisa knew for sure that this was going to be another strange conversation. "Just exactly what do you mean by that?" Lisa asked defensively.

"I mean that you told the whole world about some things that were just between friends. I asked Stevie to do me a favor and she tried, but she made a mistake. Now the whole world knows about it."

"It was *news,*" Lisa reminded her.

"But it wasn't anybody else's business!"

"Stealing is *everybody* else's business," Lisa snapped. "It happened. I didn't write anything that didn't happen."

"What you wrote made it sound like one of the girls here stole Stevie's wallet with my money in it. That's not news. It's a wild accusation!"

Lisa could now feel herself getting angry. Carole obviously just didn't understand what journalism was all about. It was her job to tell the facts. As long as she stuck to the facts, she wasn't responsible for how other people interpreted them.

"I didn't say that any of those girls stole the wallet," Lisa reminded Carole. "I just said that they were there at the time Stevie got the money. Personally, I don't have any idea who stole the wallet, but I'll tell you one thing—if my article gets the thief to return the money, you'll be thanking me, and so will everybody else."

Carole shook her head. "I suppose," she said. "But it seems a high price to pay for fifteen dollars." And then she walked off to finish tacking up her own horse.

Lisa returned her attention to Pepper. She put the saddle pad on his back, then lifted the saddle up and placed it carefully on the pad. She slid the pad and saddle into place and reached under Pepper for the girth, pulling the strap tight and fastening the first buckle.

"They just don't understand," Lisa said to Pepper.

"Journalism is reporting facts. All I did was to report the facts. I didn't say *anything* that wasn't true. And besides that, Carole's just angry because she's found out that she doesn't have any money to buy her father a present."

Lisa gave the girth a final tug as if to emphasize her statement and the piece of leather snapped in her hand. This just wasn't her day. Now she'd have to go to Mrs. Reg and get another girth. Sure as anything this would make her late for class.

The hallway in the stable area was filled with her classmates and their horses on their way to the outdoor ring. She made her way carefully among them, noting that absolutely nobody spoke to her. How different it was from what she'd been expecting that day! She'd thought everybody was going to be happy for her and proud of her. She was expecting congratulations and hugs. All she was getting was cold shoulders. She was relieved to get to Mrs. Reg's office and the tack room.

"I need a new girth," she said. "Pepper's broke." She gave Mrs. Reg the broken strap.

Mrs. Reg examined it carefully. "I just wanted to make sure somebody didn't cut it," Mrs. Reg explained.

"Who would do something like that?" Lisa asked.

"Well, you never know in a hotbed of crime like this place . . ." Mrs. Reg left the thought dangling as she found a new girth and gave it to Lisa.

Lisa took the girth, thanked Mrs. Reg, and returned to Pepper's stall. Methodically, she began to replace the old girth with the new one. She could hear the class begin in the nearby outdoor ring.

Lisa sighed. Even Mrs. Reg was annoyed with her. And that just meant that even Mrs. Reg didn't understand the responsibility of the press. She'd read about reporters who had gone to jail to protect their own rights as journalists. This wasn't exactly the same thing, but it did seem to Lisa that, like some of the finest journalists in the world, she was suffering. But suffering to protect the right of freedom of the press seemed to her like a small price to pay.

She finished buckling one side of the new girth and was about to start the second when she heard her name, from the outdoor ring.

"Where's Lisa?" Max asked the class.

"I don't know, and I don't care," somebody answered.

The words were like a slap in the face. And they proved to her that she was right. They didn't understand. But they *would* understand. No matter how difficult it was, Lisa had to continue her work. She had to make the thief realize that she wasn't going to let up until the wallet was returned.

This was no time for class, Lisa decided. She was late already, and besides, there was more news for the world to know—more to report. Quickly, she removed the saddle and bridle from Pepper, returned the tack to the tack room, changed back into her street shoes, and began the walk home.

All the way home, she was writing her next article in her head. Her friends would see. She'd make them see.

"THESE ARE SUCH silly clothes!" Trudy exclaimed, looking at herself in the dingy mirror in Pine Hollow's locker area.

Stevie laughed out loud. Trudy was dressed to go riding. She wore an old pair of her jodhpurs, low boots, and a plain blue shirt. The outfit looked very normal to Carole, especially when compared with the outfit Trudy had worn walking into the stable!

"You think *those* are funny clothes?" Carole asked.

Trudy stepped back so she could see all of herself at once in the mirror. She squinted as she examined the total effect. "Yup," she said, nodding. "They're funny all right, but I don't mind. You guys are dressed funny, too, so I don't stand out."

Carole almost took Trudy seriously until she spotted the twinkle in her eye. The idea of Trudy's being afraid to stand out in a crowd was just plain crazy. All three girls started laughing at once.

Trudy was different from anybody Carole had ever met, and she liked her a lot. She was glad Trudy was visiting Stevie, and she was particularly glad that Stevie had finally convinced Trudy to try horseback riding.

"You're going to love this," Carole assured Trudy while she handed her the tack she would need for Patch. The girls had gotten Max's permission to take Trudy on a short trail ride through some neighboring fields and a wooded area. They were under strict orders not to go faster than a walk and not to show off.

Carole didn't have to be told these things. She knew that a new rider would be safe enough, especially on a calm horse like Patch. But a calm horse could become a dangerously frisky horse if the other riders on the trail were trying stunts.

"Is my horse really big?" Trudy asked, eyeing Patch's saddle warily.

"He's big enough," Carole answered evasively. "But don't worry, you're with us. We'll take care of you."

"Riding is great—just you wait," Stevie said. "It's the most fun thing we do. You're going to love it."

Stevie had expressed Carole's feelings exactly. Riding was the greatest thing in the world as far as she was concerned. The minute Trudy was in Patch's saddle, Carole was certain she was going to see how wonderful it was.

In fact, the only thing that came close to the fun of riding itself was sharing the experience with friends. And that was the only sour note of the day: Lisa wasn't with them.

Carole and Stevie had talked about it. They were both still a little annoyed with her for writing the article about Stevie's wallet and Carole's money, but they thought Lisa had had an awful time of it on Friday and must have learned her lesson, so they wanted to make up with her. Lisa had told Carole she was really much too busy to come riding on Monday, but said she'd be at class on Tuesday as usual. It wasn't like Lisa to pass up a chance to ride. Carole was about to try to convince her to change her mind when Lisa had told her she had to go. Before Carole could say another word, Lisa had hung up.

Carole didn't know whether she was more disappointed that Lisa hadn't wanted to listen to her or that Lisa was missing from their trail ride. She did know that she felt uncomfortable with the rift. The Saddle Club was used to being united. It just didn't feel right when something came between them.

Carole finished saddling Barq. She walked him to the stable exit, fastened his lead to a cleat by the door, and helped Stevie finish saddling Patch for Trudy.

Within a few minutes, Trudy was in the saddle. Her face now had an even more pained look than it had when she'd arrived at the stables.

"The horseshoe," Stevie said. "We have to show her that. It'll make her feel better."

Carole agreed. While Trudy clung to the English saddle's abbreviated pommel, her knuckles white with the effort, Carole led Patch to the stable's good-luck horseshoe. "Touch it," Carole said. "Just touch it with your right hand. It's one of our traditions. All riders touch that before they go for a ride. No rider at Pine Hollow has ever been seriously hurt."

"There's always a first time," Trudy said, reaching tentatively for the well-worn good-luck charm.

"But it won't be today," Carole said positively, smiling encouragement at Trudy.

"Don't make fun of me," Trudy said, returning her hand to clutch the saddle.

"I'm not and I won't," Carole assured her. "Stevie and I both rode for the first time once. We were scared, too." She handed Trudy the reins. Trudy grasped them so tightly that Patch thought she was signaling to step backward. Obediently, he did so, terrorizing Trudy even more.

Carole saw what was happening and got Trudy to ease up a bit. She realized as she was doing it that Trudy really had no idea at all what she was doing. Normally, a new rider would have some sense of how to hold the reins, how to balance, how to signal the horse to go and stop. Not Trudy. She seemed as uncomfortable riding a horse as Carole thought *she* would be living in a big city.

"I think he's ready to walk someplace," Trudy said, "so we'd better get going before he changes his mind."

Carole laughed to herself, but she wasn't laughing *at* Trudy. Carole had the feeling that what Trudy really meant was that they'd better get going before *Trudy* changed her mind. Considering how much Trudy was not enjoying her ride so far, Carole found herself really admiring Trudy. She was obviously scared, but she was still willing to go ahead, just because she'd said she would give it a try. Carole thought that showed a special kind of courage.

"Yes, let's go," Carole said. She mounted Barq and touched the good-luck horseshoe herself. Stevie, who had already mounted and touched the horseshoe, was in the lead.

Carole's job was to follow. The order on a trail ride was always carefully planned. An experienced rider led the pack. The newest riders were in the middle, and another experienced rider was at the back where she or he could most easily spot trouble with the new riders. Carole was comfortable with this role, and on several occasions she'd had a chance to help a rider who needed it. In spite of Trudy's fear, Carole was quite sure that the girl's basic common sense would keep her from getting into any trouble. Anybody who was as scared as Trudy was would do anything to stay safe!

The horses ambled across one of the fields behind the stable, aimed for the woods. All three horses knew the trail well. They walked easily. The steady pace seemed to put Trudy a little bit at ease. Carole kept her eyes on Trudy, but her thoughts wandered. She thought again about Lisa and concluded that there was nothing she could do until Lisa was ready to listen. She thought about the fifteen dollars and what she was going to do about her father's birthday. That was a more serious problem. Stevie had assured her dozens of times that she'd get the money for her. She seemed convinced that it was, in fact, her fault, and she wanted to make it up to Carole and to her father.

Carole wasn't sure about either of those things. She wasn't sure it was Stevie's fault, *and* she wasn't sure Stevie would be able to come up with the money in time for the birthday. That was troublesome, but she couldn't think of a solution.

A long time ago, Carole had learned that when there was no way to solve a problem, worrying about it wasn't going to help and might just hurt. As soon as she became aware that she was worrying pointlessly, she turned her mind from Lisa and the money.

It was a lovely day, though very hot as usual for a late-summer day in Virginia. The grass in the field was high and sweet-smelling, flecked with the blossoms of wildflowers here and there. Barq reached for a bite of juicy clover. Carole shortened the reins in time to keep him from all but the smallest taste of it. It wasn't a good idea to permit a horse to munch as you rode. Between-meal snacks weren't any better for horses than they were for people. She patted him on the neck as consolation for the tasty treat he'd just missed. In front of them, Patch swished his tail first to the right, then to the left, discouraging the hungry flies from biting him. Carole smiled contentedly. There wasn't anyplace in the world she would rather have been right then than on horseback, on a scenic trail, in the sunshine.

Trudy was doing fine. In fact, she was doing better than fine. Carole noticed that her arms and legs were now relaxed. She held the reins with one hand and gestured with the other as she talked to Stevie. They were discussing hairstyles, and considering Trudy's own hairstyle, it didn't surprise Carole that Trudy needed to use wild gestures to describe them!

"How do they make the spikes stand up?" Stevie asked Trudy.

Trudy was comfortable talking about punk hairstyles, and she eagerly explained the differences between gels and mousse. Being comfortable in her conversation made her comfortable on the horse. Carole didn't think that Stevie really cared about spiking her hair. But Stevie was smart. She was putting Trudy at ease to make her more comfortable on horseback.

As they chattered on about hairstyles and eye makeup, Stevie led them through the woods and into the creekbed that ran down the sloping hillside. On a hot day, it was refreshing for the horses to splash through the water. The riders could enjoy it, too.

"Let's stop for a minute," Carole suggested. "Flat Rock's right ahead."

"Oh, great idea," Stevie agreed. "You're going to love this, Trudy!"

There was a large rock by the side of the creek where they could sit, dangle their feet in the fresh water, and cool off before the ride back.

A few minutes later, they were all enjoying the rest.

"We've got a lot of things in the city," Trudy said. "But we don't have *any*thing like this!"

"You like it?" Stevie asked.

Trudy slapped a mosquito and brushed an ant off her arm. "Well, let's just say it's different."

Stevie and Carole laughed. So did Trudy.

"You can say that again!" Stevie said, recalling the trip The Saddle Club had made to New York recently. "When we were at the American Horse Show, we got to do a lot of neat things, but we never dangled our feet in a cool stream!"

Trudy smiled. "It's probably smart to avoid any water in New York that doesn't come out of a tap," she joked.

"I mean everything about this place is different," she continued. "In the city, we don't have grass in front of everybody's house. We don't even have houses—we have apartments. Nobody's got a pool and nobody rides horses, except on the merry-go-round. We don't hang out at malls like we did yesterday, and we don't go everywhere in cars like you guys do. We ride subways and buses, and we hang out at our friends' apartments. Like I said, it's *different*."

"This is better, isn't it?" Stevie asked. She was excited to have a chance to show off Willow Creek and horseback riding to Trudy. She wanted Trudy to like them as much as she did.

"I'm having a good time, Stevie, I really am. But the city is home. I like the city. I even miss it a bit."

"Oh," Stevie said. She couldn't think of anything else to say. Trudy had surprised her. Stevie wouldn't have thought that anybody would prefer living in a city to living in the country and being able to ride.

"I think I know what you mean," Carole said. "As a Marine Corps brat, I've lived in a lot of different places. Each was different, but each was home, too. And home is nice, whatever it is. Right?"

"Something like that," Trudy agreed. "But I'll tell you one thing. Two weeks ago, I wouldn't have thought anybody could ever get me up on a horse. No way, nohow. Now that I've done it, I wonder why I was so scared. Horses are okay."

"Okay" wasn't the word either Stevie or Carole would have used, but considering where Trudy had started less than an hour ago, that sounded like a major endorsement of horseback riding. Carole and Stevie were satisfied with Trudy's progress.

"If we don't get you back on time, Max will send out a search party," Carole said, giving the cool water a final smack with her bare foot. Stevie glanced at her watch. It was definitely time to go. The three girls put their boots back on and had a nicely uneventful ride back to Pine Hollow.

As far as Stevie and Carole were concerned, the

only thing wrong with the whole ride was that Lisa hadn't been along to enjoy it with them.

WHILE HER FRIENDS were riding in the woods with Trudy, Lisa was very busy. She had a deadline to meet. As before, most of her article concerned the routine events at Pine Hollow. She wrote about the stable's newest horse, Topside, which Max had bought from one of his ex-students, champion Dorothy DeSoto, and about the class of youngest riders. They were working on mounting and dismounting by themselves from the mounting block. Then she got to the real news.

After last week's news about the theft at Pine Hollow was reported, many other incidents of apparent theft have come to light to this reporter. At least one riding hat was stolen, as well as a pair of expensive riding gloves, a riding crop, and a set of keys. Since these thefts took place at different times, it is difficult to determine whether they were all done by the same thief or several. One thing is certain: Young riders at Pine Hollow must watch their personal property carefully!

Lisa leaned back from her desk and reread the words she'd written. It was true. Every word of it. That was what journalists were supposed to do. They were supposed to write what was true.

She was a journalist.

8

STEVIE AND CAROLE talked to one another on the phone early on Friday—as soon as each of them had read Lisa's latest column.

"I can't believe it," Carole said. "It's worse than the last one!"

"She's going to be in *so* much trouble—and she's making trouble for everybody else. She makes Pine Hollow sound like a den of thieves!"

"We've got to talk some sense into her," said Carole.

"You can only talk to somebody who's listening," Stevie said. "And the last time I talked to her about her column, I can tell you, she wasn't listening."

"That must have been the time she said that you and I 'didn't understand the principles of journalism.'"

"Either then, or the time she was sure that anybody who criticized her was just jealous of her success."

Carole shook her head. "It's just not like Lisa to be so stubborn."

"You're right about that. There's just no talking to her at all."

"It doesn't mean we shouldn't try," Carole said.

Stevie agreed. It was clear that something had to be done, and it was going to be better if Lisa's friends did it. She and Carole discussed the best approach.

According to her mother's magazines, Stevie told Carole, this situation called for the careful use of *psychology*. Carole was ready to try it a few hours later when they all met at the stable.

LISA HOPED THAT her riding classmates would receive her second effort better than they had her first. She thought that by now they would be getting used to the idea that a reporter tried to right wrongs. And certainly riding clothes and wallets being stolen qualified as wrongs.

The first thing she saw when she approached Pine Hollow Friday morning was that Carole, Stevie, and Trudy were standing outside, apparently waiting for her. She smiled tentatively, hoping she'd find them glad to see her. They waved. Lisa breathed a sigh of relief.

"How did you like my new column?" she asked. She just couldn't wait to hear what they thought.

"Oh, it was just great!" Carole said.

"I loved the part about Topside," Stevie said.

Lisa had known Stevie would like that. Stevie loved Topside. She smiled, pleased with herself.

"And I liked reading about the youngest class here," Trudy said. "They already know more than I do!"

Lisa laughed. Then she realized that her friends weren't talking about the meaty part of her article. "And the things about the robberies?" she asked.

"Well," Carole began. "We think there's a little problem there—or at least *could* be."

Lisa didn't like the sound of this. "Just what does *that* mean?"

"It kind of sounds like you think there are a lot of things being stolen at Pine Hollow," Stevie said.

"But it's true!" Lisa defended herself.

"How do you know?" Trudy challenged her.

"Because people told me," Lisa said.

She was so disappointed. Here she was, talking with her very best friends—the ones she thought she could count on to be happy for her, to be proud of her—and all they wanted to do was to criticize her! They were just as jealous as all the other girls in the stable!

Stevie knew right away that they'd made a mistake. They'd agreed to tell Lisa what was good about her column before they tried to tell her what was wrong with it, but the wrong-with-it part wasn't going to sink in. All they'd managed to do was to hurt her feelings and make her defensive. The look on their friend's face told the whole story.

"Hey, Lisa," Stevie said, trying to change the subject smoothly. "Carole and I are going to work with Samson for a while before class. Want to help?"

"Right, I could use some help," Carole added.

"No thank you," Lisa said coolly. "I need to get ready for class, and besides, I've got to make some notes for my next column. I've got a deadline, you know."

The chill in her voice said everything her words didn't. Stevie knew that for then, at least, there was nothing else to say. She told Lisa they'd see her in class, and she and Carole and Trudy left to work with Samson. Stevie was eager to get out of Lisa's way. She didn't want to be on Lisa's mind when Lisa was working on her column!

As soon as they'd left, Lisa went to the locker area. She did want to make some notes, but she didn't want to do it with her friends butting in. She'd had enough advice for one day. Working in front of anybody else would just invite more.

She sat on the end of the bench in the locker area and reached down into the bottom of her backpack. She had brought something very special—a miniature tape recorder so she could just talk into it when she thought of something she wanted to include in her next column. She clicked the RECORD button and began talking.

"Trudy," she said. Then she clicked off the machine. She thought Trudy was interesting and she wanted to write about her. It was easy for people to make judgments about others based on how they looked. But it was clear there was more to Trudy than that. Just by saying her name onto the tape, Lisa was reminding herself to think about what she wanted to write.

At that moment, the subject of her thoughts returned to the locker area.

"Do you know where I can find a lead rope?" Trudy asked. "If Carole ever catches Samson," she explained with a grin, "she wants to try to lead him around. Personally, I think Samson is having too much fun playing tag to want to be led anywhere!"

"There's a hook on the wall over there," Lisa said, pointing into the tack room. "You can take any one of them. They're all the same."

"Thanks," Trudy said, and turned to follow Lisa's directions. She paused, then turned back to Lisa. "You working on another column?" she asked, obviously noticing the tape recorder.

"Yes, I am," Lisa said cautiously. "I use this to make notes to myself—reminders, really, of things I want to write about. It's the sort of thing we reporters do."

"I think what you're doing is very interesting," Trudy said.

"You do?" Lisa said, surprised. This was the first time anybody had expressed any interest in what she was doing. "Everybody else is just angry with me. Jealous, you know."

"No, I think it's interesting," Trudy said. "Nobody from my neighborhood could do that, you know."

"Really? You mean nobody there has the writing talent? I'm sure if they tried—maybe even you . . ."

Trudy shook her head, making her dangly white and purple earrings click and clatter. "That's not what I mean. I think it's a city-country thing."

That didn't sound right to Lisa and she told Trudy so. "But the greatest newspapers in the world are in big cities! Investigative reporting began in a big city. For me, this is just practice, until I get my shot at a *real* newspaper. How can you say this wouldn't happen in a city?"

"I guess I'm not saying this right," Trudy said. "You see, I don't think what you're doing could happen in my neighborhood. In the city, everybody lives very close to everybody else. Here, your neighbors are across a driveway and a garage, maybe a hedge or a flower patch or even a big lawn. Where I'm from, your neighbors are across the hall, maybe on the other side of a wall. You sneeze, they say 'Gesundheit.'"

Lisa grinned.

"We don't all like each other, but we get along by minding our own business most of the time. It's a way of adding space between people who are really crowded together. I get along with all my friends because if I see something somebody didn't want me to see, or if somebody tells me something, I *don't* tell. I guess because there's really no privacy, you've got to pretend by minding your own business. But out here, it seems, you've got the real space between you, and that makes it real different. You can go ahead and write about private things you only learned because you are somebody's friend. Things that they might not have said if they'd known you were going to write about it. I guess it's just different."

"Oh," Lisa said, disappointed to learn that Trudy apparently wanted to criticize her, too. She'd thought she was going to get genuine admiration from Trudy, but what she'd gotten was just another lecture from somebody else who didn't understand what real journalism was all about: to report the truth.

"Trudy! Did you get lost?" Stevie walked into the locker area.

"Oh, no," Trudy said. "I was just talking with Lisa. Sorry." Quickly, Trudy walked over to the hook where the lead ropes hung, selected one, and followed Stevie out the door toward the paddock. "See you, Lisa," Trudy said.

Lisa listened to the footsteps receding down the stable's hallway and sighed. They hadn't even invited her to join them. It seemed to be her fate to be misunderstood.

A horse was led past the door to the locker area. That reminded Lisa that before her own class started, Max was giving a private lesson to a beginner. He'd told her she could observe the class for her column. She liked the idea; it would be good for her readers to be able to compare the beginners' group class she'd written about this week with a beginner's private lesson. Quickly, she shoved her things back into her cubby, taking only a pad and pen with her. She would distract Max and the rider if she whispered into the recorder during the lesson.

Lisa thought it was a great idea to be getting back to work. It seemed that the longer she sat in the locker area, the greater risk she had of getting another lecture about how to write a column for the newspaper. Besides, the smell of paint was giving her a headache.

9

"Now the secret to looking cool is being able to coordinate really different things," Trudy explained to Stevie and Carole, boldly leading the way through the accessories department of My Way, a clothing store at the local mall.

Trudy picked up one oversize scarf after another, examined each quickly, and tossed each back into the bin. "Not right, maybe—ugh! No way . . ." she said.

Stevie held a blouse Trudy had already chosen. It was hot pink, buttoned down the back, and was sleeveless with a mock turtleneck. Stevie thought it was very stylish as it was. The scarf Trudy held had some of the same hot pink in it—in blotches. There were also blotches of about forty other colors.

"This is really too go-with-everything," Trudy said, dropping the latest candidate. "See, what I have in mind is to wear this blouse with my camouflage pants. The scarf I buy will have to bring the two pieces together."

"About the only thing that can bring this blouse together with a pair of camouflage pants is a can of paint," Stevie said, thinking out loud.

Trudy's eyes flashed with amusement. "Just you wait and see," she said. "You'll love it."

"You're not going to make me wear this outfit when you put it together, are you?" Stevie asked.

"I won't have to make you wear it," Trudy said. "You'll beg me to borrow it!"

"For the Mardi Gras costume party?" Carole teased.

Trudy laughed. "You'll see," she repeated, then went back to her furious search.

Stevie watched, fascinated. She couldn't remember when she'd had more fun at the mall or looking for clothes than she and Carole were having that afternoon with Trudy. She and Carole and Lisa had visited the mall many times, but it seemed that they always visited the same stores and looked at the same things—or at least the same kinds of things. Going to the mall with Trudy meant seeing things she'd never seen before. It would never have occurred to her to buy a pair of camouflage pants. She hadn't even known where they were sold. She did now. She'd also learned where she could buy sandals with straps that wrapped all the way up her legs to above her knees.

She hadn't bought any of these things, of course, but Trudy had. And Trudy just loved them.

There was a more serious side to Trudy, too, though. As soon as she'd seen the card table at the mall entrance where the library's raffle tickets were being sold, she'd insisted on buying a whole book of them. She didn't care about the prizes; she just wanted to be helpful. Carole and Stevie were both happy she wanted to give money to their town library.

Stevie glanced over to where Trudy was dancing around the scarf bin, humming to herself, and grinned. Sometimes it could be boring going shopping with somebody and not buying anything for herself, but being with Trudy was such an experience that Stevie didn't mind at all. Being with Trudy meant shopping for things she'd never buy—but it was fun! It was obvious that Carole felt exactly the same way she did. She, too, was watching Trudy's quest with rapt fascination.

"I think I like having a sister," Stevie confided to Carole. "Trudy's a lot more fun than all three of my brothers put together."

"That's not much of a contest," Carole remarked. "I don't think I remember you ever saying a thing about your brothers being any fun at all."

"They aren't."

Trudy pulled a scarf out of the box. It was actually olive green and hot pink.

"Yeah!" she announced to everybody within earshot. "Now I've just got to try it on!" Stevie was carrying the bag with the camouflage pants in it. Trudy grabbed it from her hand, took the pink blouse as well, and ran off to find a dressing room.

"You know, she reminds me of Samson," Stevie remarked, watching Trudy wind through the shop in search of a dressing room.

"Sort of like a kid, you mean?" Carole asked.

"Yeah, I guess," Stevie said. "You know—if you let Samson do what he wants, he's just so funny! Trudy's the same way. She's always up to something."

"Yeah, I know exactly what you mean. Samson's just crazy . . . Hey, wait a minute!" Carole said, regarding Stevie carefully. "What did you mean when you said the thing about letting Samson do what he wants?"

Stevie shrugged. "Every time he does something, it's like another game. He really loves them. I started to teach him things like peekaboo and tag, but it was like he already knew them. He's a riot—just like Trudy." Stevie looked at Carole and saw the very odd look on her face. "Well, not exactly like Trudy," she said. "But you know, fun loving."

"You mean, you *taught* him those games?" Carole asked, suddenly beginning to understand what might have been going on.

"I hardly had to teach him," Stevie said. "He's a natural. I was going to put the halter on him, see, and we just got to playing . . ."

78

"But Stevie, you couldn't do that!" Carole exclaimed.

"Sure I could. It was *easy!*" Stevie said.

"Of course it was easy," Carole said, taking a deep breath to calm herself. "You wanted to play, he wanted to play. The trouble is that you went in there with a halter and instead of working with him, you let him play. Now every time somebody goes in with a halter, all he wants to do is to play."

"And he's so cute!" Stevie said.

Carole realized that Stevie still didn't understand what had happened.

"Sure he's cute, but he's got a job to do. When you're teaching a horse something, you have to stick to the work or else he'll get the idea that playing is okay. Horses forget what they learn very quickly unless you keep reminding them, just like little kids."

"You mean I shouldn't have played with him?"

"Not with a halter in your hand—especially not with one that he hadn't already put on. It's like you rewarded him for misbehaving. It's not that he's ruined for life or anything, but it means we have to begin at the beginning again and make him unlearn all the games just like he unlearned his manners."

"Aw, come on, Carole. Are you trying to tell me that I can't play games with Samson?" Stevie put her hands on her hips and glared at Carole. "He's not just your horse, you know."

Carole returned the glare. "Games should be a reward for work *well* done, not a reward for work *un-*done!"

"You're making a federal case out of this," Stevie said.

Carole could tell Stevie was getting angry. She didn't care. *She* was angry with Stevie for being so thoughtless about working with the foal. "I'm not making a federal case," Carole retorted. "I'm just telling you the facts. You didn't want to work with Samson at all. You just wanted to play with him."

"Yeah, and you're just jealous of all the fun I had. *That's* what's going on!"

"Jealous? Who's jealous?" Trudy asked, walking up to where Carole and Stevie were standing facing one another angrily. "Are you talking about Lisa? Because although I don't know her really well, I think she's okay and something's going to make her see that what she's doing isn't cool."

"We're not talking about Lisa," Stevie said, still looking straight at Carole. "We're talking about Carole. See, she's telling me that what I did, playing games with Samson, was bad to do, and I think she's just jealous because I had so much fun! What do *you* think?"

Both Carole and Stevie looked at Trudy and for the first time, noticed that she was wearing her new outfit.

"*I* think this scarf was exactly what I needed," Trudy said, pirouetting so they could admire the effect.

Both were surprised. Trudy was wearing the camouflage pants and the hot-pink blouse. She also had the
scarf on, but was wearing it as a belt. The outfit was as
flamboyant as anything either had ever seen, but on
Trudy, it worked. "Now . . . if I can get some hair
color to highlight the hot pink. Then . . . ooh, I
think I remember seeing some earrings made of empty
shell casings. I think they're in the shop we passed
when we first came into the mall. What do you think
for shoes?"

"Flats," Stevie suggested.

Trudy nodded. "Either that or combat boots."

Carole couldn't control it anymore. She started
laughing. So did Stevie. Trudy laughed, too. When
they'd all recovered, Trudy returned to the dressing
room and changed back into her own clothes. Then
Carole led the way to the check-out counter so Trudy
could pay for her new outfit.

"I don't know how you do it," Stevie said as they
waited in line, aware of the stares of other shoppers
who noticed Trudy—what she was wearing and what
she was buying to wear. "That's the weirdest outfit I
ever saw, but on you, it's almost cute. How did you
learn to dress like that?"

"My mother taught me," Trudy said.

"I can't believe that," said Stevie. "I've met your
mother, remember? I saw her at my mother's office last
year. Your mother is the most normal dresser I ever saw.
I think she was wearing a pinstripe suit when I saw her.
And maybe one of those little bow-tie things."

Trudy plunked her clothes on the counter and fished her wallet out of the mini–duffel bag that served as her pocketbook. "That's what I mean. See, my mother would *like* me to dress just like Lisa—everything matched and tailored. But one day, while she was picking out some plaid skirts and pastel blouses, I went into the Surplus Shop and found this really neat coverall outfit. I spent my money on that instead of the skirt and blouse she was choosing for me. One taste of punk and I knew I'd found my style. If my mother hadn't let me buy my own clothes, I might never have known."

The salesclerk began adding up Trudy's purchases. Stevie turned to Carole. "I think there's a lesson there," she said, grinning.

Carole cocked her head. "What do you mean?"

Stevie continued her thought. "Well, if I let Samson choose what he wants to do instead of making him do what I know he has to do . . ."

Carole nodded, hoping her point had finally gotten through to Stevie.

". . . Samson will end up dying his mane olive and hot pink, and wearing a camouflage saddle."

"Right, and all the other horses will be jealous," Carole added before bursting into laughter.

Trudy took her change and picked up her bag. "Come on," she said. "I remember where I saw the shell-casing earrings. While we walk over there, you tell me what's so funny."

"Only if you'll tell us how to make spikes in a horse's mane," Stevie said, following her happily.

Carole walked between the two of them, slinging her arms across her friends' shoulders. "What about horseshoe earrings for Samson?" she asked.

THIS TIME, LISA was sure everybody would be happy. There was a special spring in her step as she walked toward the stable the next Friday. She hadn't said a word in her column about anything's being taken from anybody. She hadn't said anything that could possibly point a finger at anybody in the stable. She'd included the usual things Mr. Teller made her include about who had learned proper reining techniques in the beginner class and who had jumped for the first time. And then she'd gotten to the good stuff.

She'd devoted all the rest of her column to Trudy. Trudy, she thought, was a very interesting person, and she wanted everybody else to know it, too. She'd written about how she dressed in such a unique manner, of course, but there was more than that to Trudy, and she'd covered that in her column. She'd written about how great it was to have Trudy visit Willow Creek and how much fun the riders were having with her there. She'd written about how Trudy was adjusting to the country and how different it was, just the way Trudy had told her when they'd been in the locker area. In spite of the fact that Trudy had sort of butted her nose in, Lisa liked Trudy, and this column was her way of introducing Trudy to everybody who might not have a chance to meet her during her short stay in Willow Creek.

This time, Lisa was sure, everybody was going to be happy with what she'd written. She was already planning her next column, too. She had the idea of writing an article comparing adult classes with her group's classes, and she needed to ask Mrs. Reg about it. So, instead of going right into the locker area, she veered off at Mrs. Reg's office first.

Mrs. Reg's office had two doors—one from the stable's hallway and one that opened into the tack room. The far end of the tack room was the locker area. Usually, Mrs. Reg could be found in her office or the tack room, but there was no sign of her right then. Lisa only had about fifteen minutes until class started so she couldn't go on a big hunt for Mrs. Reg. Hurriedly, she scribbled a note, asking Mrs. Reg when she could observe one of Max's adult classes, then headed for the locker area.

Something stopped her, however, before she left Mrs. Reg's office. That something was the sound of her own name on Veronica diAngelo's lips.

"Lisa's done it again, you guys—only this time, I think she's right on target!"

"Oh, shut up, Veronica!" came the familiar sound of Stevie's voice.

"Listen to this," Veronica said. From where Lisa stood in the shadows inside Mrs. Reg's office, Lisa could see Veronica. She'd just climbed up onto one of the freshly painted narrow benches in front of the cubbies. She held a piece of paper in her hand. Lisa recognized it as a newspaper clipping, and from the ad on the back, she realized it was a copy of her article. Veronica diAngelo was going to read Hoof Beat out loud.

Something was wrong. Of all the people who would want to meet Trudy, the last in the world was Veronica. Veronica was a snob and she didn't want to meet anybody who wasn't in her own class—social class, that was. Trudy was neat, but Veronica would never consider her good enough. Could it be that Lisa had descibed her so well that Veronica was interested? It didn't seem likely.

"'There's a new face at the stable these days—a *very* different face!'" Veronica read Lisa's words. The girls in Veronica's group laughed. The way Veronica said it made it sound like an insult. That wasn't what Lisa had written; at least it wasn't what she'd meant to write. "'By chance and good fortune, Trudy Sanders has come to visit. She is staying with the Lake family.'" Veronica looked up from the paper to her listeners. "Whose good fortune?" she asked. The girls laughed again.

"Veronica, stop it!" Stevie said. "You're making fun of Trudy."

"I am not," Veronica said. "I'm just reading a newspaper article, straight out of *The Willow Creek Gazette*. Finally Lisa is writing something I can believe in!"

"Don't be such a jerk," Stevie said, standing up. "Trudy's in Topside's stall, right across the hall, currying him until she can come watch our class." Lisa realized then that Trudy was so close she had to be able to hear every word. It made Lisa feel awful.

"But she's your friend, isn't she?" Veronica taunted. "Some friend."

Stevie was one of the most loyal people Lisa knew. Of course she would stand up for Trudy, no matter how bad Veronica made her sound.

"Yes, Lisa is my friend," Stevie said. "And she's a great friend, too. She's trying hard to do something important, and even though she's making some mistakes . . ."

Stevie went on, but Lisa didn't hear her words because her meaning was sinking in. Stevie wasn't defending *Trudy*. Veronica had been mocking her, *Lisa*.

Even after Stevie had finished and stormed out to tack up Comanche for class, Lisa was still frozen in place, hiding in the shadows of Mrs. Reg's office. She heard the rest of Veronica's presentation, too. Veronica continued to read Lisa's article, but now the words didn't sound like hers and the message certainly wasn't the one she wanted to convey. Instead of describing the Trudy she knew and really liked, she listened to words that seemed to insult Trudy, as if she weren't really as good as the girls of Willow Creek. Some of it was the way Veronica read, but a lot of the problem came directly from the words Lisa had written.

"'For Trudy, this visit to Willow Creek is an escape from the dingy city, where neighbors crowd upon one another . . .'"

Lisa realized with a start that that made it sound as if Trudy lived in a rat-infested slum, but that wasn't the case at all. Lisa felt a blush of shame rise. Could she really have written those words?

"'And of course, the most noteworthy aspect of Trudy Sanders is her unique wardrobe! Bright colors mix freely—even within her unusual hairdos! And when she matches her orange hair with some orange eyeshadow—look out!'"

Veronica and her friends laughed hysterically. Lisa didn't know whether they were laughing harder at her or at Trudy, and she didn't care. She'd made Trudy seem like a freak, not like the nice girl she was. How could she have done that to Trudy—and how could she have done that to herself? She felt she deserved all the mocking laughter Veronica and her pals could hand out, but it wasn't fair for them to laugh at Trudy for what Lisa had done.

"Isn't it wonderful?" Veronica asked her friends when she'd finished reading the column. "I'm so glad Lisa is writing this column now. At first, I wasn't sure, but this—*this*"—she started laughing and waved the column in the air—"makes all the trouble of the last few weeks worthwhile. Maybe next week she'll do a job on one of her other friends—if she has any left!"

Lisa could tell Veronica was just warming up to her subject and had lots more to say when she was interrupted by the public address system. Max announced that class would begin in five minutes. The girls hurried to collect their tack and go saddle their horses.

Lisa remained in Mrs. Reg's office, hiding in the shadows, unable to move. Thoughts raced through her mind, the words that Veronica had read echoing again and again. Everything that had sounded so cute and funny when she'd written it had come out sounding cruel and heartless as Veronica read it. True, Veronica could make a Valentine sound like a death threat, but the words were Lisa's. She'd written everything Veronica had read, and although she hadn't meant to at all, she'd made Trudy sound awful. Poor Trudy.

"Lisa, is that you?" Mrs. Reg's soft voice broke into her thoughts. "Are you crying, dear?"

Lisa brushed her cheek with her hand and was surprised to find it streaked with tears. She hadn't realized. She knew that they were tears of anger, tears of humiliation, tears of sadness, but mostly, they were tears for Trudy. She must have hurt Trudy very much and that was exactly the opposite of what she'd meant to do.

Then she could see what Trudy had been telling her. Friends don't treat one another the way she'd been treating her friends. They don't take things said in private and make them public the way she'd done with Trudy; they don't use others' personal problems for their own personal use, the way she'd done with the loss of Stevie's wallet. That wasn't what friendship was about; it also wasn't what journalism was about. She wasn't being a journalist, she was just being a gossip.

Mrs. Reg slipped her arm across Lisa's shoulder to comfort her. Lisa had the feeling Mrs. Reg knew exactly what had happened. Mrs. Reg always seemed to know.

"Oh," Lisa said, turning to the older woman, "Mrs. Reg, I've done the most awful thing!"

Mrs. Reg hugged her and then Lisa's tears came pouring out. On top of everything else, she didn't feel as if she deserved Mrs. Reg's comfort. That made her cry even harder.

"I've hurt so many people's feelings," she said. "I hurt Stevie and Carole and Anna, Betsy, and Polly— even Veronica—and now worst of all, I hurt Trudy's. I didn't mean to do it, but I did it. Everything I wrote was worse than the last thing I'd done. I'm just so awful!" She wanted to say more, but she was crying too hard.

Mrs. Reg reached for a tissue from the top of her desk and gave it to Lisa. Then a second and a third. She waited, quietly, until finally the last tear had dropped.

"Done?" Mrs. Reg asked.

Lisa nodded. "Definitely! I'm done writing, I'm done with my friends, I guess I'm even done riding."

"Hold on now," Mrs. Reg said. "Just because you've made a whole bunch of mistakes doesn't mean it's time to make a whole bunch more." Mrs. Reg led Lisa to the tack room bench where they both sat down. "I remember a rider we had here once," she began.

Mrs. Reg was famous for her memory of past horses and riders. It seemed to The Saddle Club that whenever there was a problem, Mrs. Reg had a story to tell. Lisa and her friends had learned long ago that her stories were usually worth listening to.

"This rider started riding here when she was about your age, but she'd already been riding for years. Max knew right away that she had talent, but she also had problems. Lots of them. See, not only had she been riding for years, but she'd been riding wrong for years. She wanted to be a championship rider and Max thought she could be among the best. That was the only place they agreed. See, she'd gotten the idea that her job, as a rider, was to control the horse. From the minute she'd get into the saddle until she got out, she held that poor animal in check, tugging on the reins, squeezing him with her legs, hitting him with the whip. He'd usually do what she wanted because he knew she was the boss."

"Isn't the rider supposed to be the boss?" Lisa asked.

"Yes and no," Mrs. Reg said. "The rider certainly needs to establish who's in charge, but once that's clear, the object should be to work together. If the rider spends all the time controlling, then there's no time to cooperate. It works and there's no question that you can ride that way, but it's no way to be a champion."

"I bet Max didn't like her being so mean to his horses," Lisa said. "Did he refuse to let her ride here?"

"Oh, no," Mrs. Reg said. "He knew she was going to be a good rider and he wanted to work with her, so he started her from the beginning. First, he had her work with all the horses on a lead rope, then a lunge line. That gave them more freedom and let her learn what they could do without her legs and whip. Also, he had her give them carrots every time they did something right for her."

"Was that sort of an apology to the horses?" Lisa asked.

"Exactly," Mrs. Reg said. "When she'd made friends with the horses, she actually began liking them and trusting them. So he started her in a beginner's class and taught her from scratch."

"Oh, she must have been so bored!" Lisa said.

"Not at all," Mrs. Reg said. "See, you're only bored when you're studying things you already know. She *was* a beginner. Almost nothing she'd done before was going to be of any use to her. She had to work very hard."

Mrs. Reg stood up as if to dismiss Lisa. As usual, her story was ending before her listener was ready for the end. Lisa stood up, too.

"So what happened then?"

Mrs. Reg looked at her as if she were a little surprised that Lisa didn't already know the answer. "Why, she became a champion, of course. Now, if you see Red, tell him I need him. He's just got to get on with the painting. Can you believe the smell? I can't stand it. I'm sure the horses can't either. And I also have to call the grain and feed man . . ." Mrs. Reg strode into her office and picked up the phone. Lisa was left alone with her thoughts.

Since Mrs. Reg's stories were usually lessons in disguise, Lisa's next step was to figure out just what the lesson was. Obviously, she had to learn something about journalism from the very beginning. She was a long way from being ready for a job as an investigative reporter. But first, what did the lead rope and the lunge line and the carrots have to do with journalism?

Then she understood. Just as the championship rider had to apologize to the horses she'd hurt before she could begin again, she, Lisa, had to apologize to the people she'd hurt before she could learn anything about writing. She had hurt a lot of people, she knew, but the one she'd hurt most had been Trudy. That was the place to start.

It was too late for her to join the class now, and besides, Lisa didn't want to face any of her classmates just yet. The most important thing was to find Trudy and talk to her.

Lisa shoved her things into her cubby and headed for the outdoor ring where the class was taking place. Trudy liked to sit on the fence and observe, but Lisa could see from inside the stable that Trudy wasn't there. She checked Samson and Delilah's paddock. No sign of her. She looked in the feed room, Max's office, the stalls, and the tack room. Trudy was nowhere to be found.

"Trudy?" Red said when Lisa asked. "I think she's having a private lesson. She asked me to show her how to tack up Topside."

"Trudy?" one of the painters said when Lisa stopped him. "The one with the colored hair? I saw her riding by herself out toward the trails."

By herself? Trudy didn't have anywhere near enough experience to ride by herself. What could she have been thinking of? Lisa wondered.

Then Lisa knew: Trudy was running away, the only way she could think of—on horseback.

Lisa guessed that Trudy had waited until the class was in progress before taking Topside out of the stable. Everybody would be too busy then to notice.

Lisa knew that Trudy could be in real danger out there by herself. An inexperienced rider had no business on the trails alone. Even on a gentle horse Trudy could be in real trouble. Topside wasn't a gentle horse. He was a champion show horse—spirited and determined. Trudy Sanders was no match for him.

Lisa knew that she could ask Max for help, or Mrs. Reg or Red or any other rider. She also knew that she was the reason Trudy was gone, and she would be the reason Trudy would come back.

11

LISA HAD NEVER saddled her horse faster than she did that day. Pepper seemed to understand that this was no day to play games. He stood completely still and even lowered his head so she could put the bridle on. She patted him in thanks, remembering Mrs. Reg's story.

Lisa led her horse to the stable exit out of sight of the outdoor ring and mounted him. She didn't want her classmates or Max to see that she was going out by herself. Obviously Trudy must have done the same thing. That meant that she had at least started out on one of the trails that began at the back of the stable. Lisa began to consider the options before she realized she had forgotten something very important. She had forgotten the good-luck horseshoe.

She turned Pepper back toward the stable, walked

him up to the doorway, and brushed the horseshoe with her hand. Then she was ready to begin her quest.

But which trail? Sitting tall on Pepper's back, she surveyed the possibilities. All of the Pine Hollow students knew the trails because they'd ridden them time and time again. There were four starting at the back of the stable that Trudy might have taken. First was Lisa's favorite, the mountain trail, which led into the woods and up the mountain. Then, the forest trail. It headed straight for the mountain and wound through the woods. The creek trail started out on a hill and followed the creek that gave Willow Creek its name. Finally, there was the field trail. It snaked through nearby fields, running into the woods parallel to the river that Willow Creek became. Beyond it was the highway. Until it got into the woods, it wasn't a very pretty trail—certainly Lisa's least favorite.

Lisa decided on the mountain trail and signaled Pepper to head to the left when something occurred to her. Trudy was a city girl. She *liked* concrete, especially the kind that could be found on the highway. If she was actually running away, she'd know that the highway could lead her home.

There were two problems with that. The first was that the river was deep, wide, and dangerous at the point where the trail reached it. The other was that it was right next to the highway where trucks honked, cars backfired, and sirens sometimes wailed. Topside was a champion, but he was also skittish. Highway noises could frighten Topside and Trudy wasn't experienced enough to control him. Lisa realized she didn't have a minute to spare.

She turned Pepper toward the field trail. "Come on, boy," she said. "We've got a job to do!"

Pepper seemed to understand her. His ears perked up alertly. He tensed, ready for her next instruction. She nudged him in the belly and shifted her weight forward in the saddle. Pepper broke into a fast walk, and when he was warmed up, Lisa got him to trot and then canter. It was the best chance for Lisa to catch up with Trudy before she got into trouble. Unless Topside got out of control, Trudy was too inexperienced to do more than walk him.

The grass in the fields had been cut for the harvest so Lisa could see clearly around her. She kept a sharp eye for anything suspicious in the grass and was relieved when there was nothing to see.

If she'd been able to travel straight to the creek, it would have been only about a mile, about a ten-minute ride. But the hilly fields made it impossible to go straight and she had to follow the trail. It took her more than forty-five minutes to reach the final hillock. When she crested it, she found Trudy.

Her first instinct was to laugh at the sight, a hundred yards away down the hill on the edge of the river. There stood the city girl, sopping wet and hopping mad. Her usually stand-up hairdo hung limply on her neck. The pinkish dye she'd sprayed on that morning had seeped onto her yellow shirt. But the funny part of the scene was the fact that Trudy was standing almost toe-to-toe with Topside, hands on her hips, and her chin jutted out in the most determinedly stubborn look Lisa had ever seen as she concentrated on her battle of wits with the horse. Topside wasn't budging. He returned her glare with a bored stare. As Lisa watched, Trudy made what looked like an attempt at delivering the last word and walked around to the horse's left side, picking up the reins. She was ready to mount. She was following all the instructions Carole and Stevie had apparently given her because she was making a good start. But as soon as she lifted her left foot to put it in the stirrup, Topside took two steps to the right, leaving Trudy unbalanced with her foot in the air. She fell down.

Lisa giggled. Then she realized it wasn't really a funny scene, certainly not to Trudy, who had experienced enough unhappiness for one day. Trudy must have attempted to cross the river and Topside had thrown her. The horse understood that the minute Trudy got back on him, she was going to try again. He didn't want to cross the river. The easiest way for him was to not let her mount.

There was no telling how long the standoff could have gone on. Lisa noticed that the whole time, Topside's ears were twitching alertly, aware of the noises of the highway. One honk and he'd take off. The risks were too great that he'd hurt Trudy when he did it.

Lisa gave Pepper a signal to continue. The hill was steep and he had to go slowly, step by step. The delay worried Lisa. She had the feeling that Trudy needed her help a lot more than Trudy realized.

As Lisa watched with concern, Trudy once more took the reins. This time, however, instead of moving slowly toward the championship horse, she dashed up to the horse's left side and sprang upward, clinging to his saddle for all she was worth. Topside took off at a trot. Trudy held on, somehow managing to get into the saddle. She even got one foot into his stirrups.

"Hold on!" Lisa cried, now close enough to be heard. "You're doing great!"

Trudy glanced at her. Her surprise was apparent, but her fear—and anger—was even more obvious.

"Leave me alone!" Trudy yelled back at her. "You've done enough harm already! Go away!"

In her agitation, Trudy yanked at Topside's reins. The motion was sudden and firm and gave a clear message to the horse. Topside halted immediately.

Lisa sighed with relief.

A passing eighteen-wheel truck blasted its horn and Topside took off at full speed.

Trudy was jostled so badly that the one foot that was in a stirrup slipped through it. Now she had lost any chance to use her feet for balance, and Lisa knew that she was at a very definite risk of being thrown by Topside. If that happened when her foot was sticking all the way through the stirrup, she could be dragged along by the horse.

There wasn't a second to lose! Once again, Pepper understood her urgency.

"Grab his mane, hold on!" Lisa cried, knowing that if she held the mane tight, Trudy had a chance of keeping her balance. Topside swerved to the right, Trudy lurched to the left, her left foot dangling treacherously through the stirrup.

Pepper galloped along the hillside, parallel to the runaway horse, but well above him. There was no way Pepper could gallop *down* the hill. It was an extremely dangerous thing for a horse to do. Lisa just had to stay as close as possible until the hill flattened out in another hundred yards.

"I can't control him!" Trudy yelled.

"Don't worry, I'll be there as fast as I can. Just hold on!" Lisa yelled.

She tried to sound confident. She didn't feel it at all. She just hoped that Trudy didn't realize what a dangerous situation she was in. The last thing Trudy needed was to get more panicky than she was.

Lisa felt as if it were almost a dream, as if she were watching the action from very far away. She was aware of the horses, racing along the riverbank. She felt the power of the horse beneath her, she heard the thunderous clamor of hoofbeats, but the only thing she saw, really saw, was Trudy's foot dangling through Topside's stirrup. It drove her as she had never known she could be driven. Slowly, achingly slowly, she got Pepper to move downhill, closer to Topside, closer to the dangling foot. "Hold on," she whispered in her horse's ear. "Hold on. Don't let go of the mane. Don't fall. I'll get there. Please be okay . . ."

Pepper didn't understand the words, but certainly he knew the urgency in Lisa's commands. He lengthened his stride and moved farther down the hill, nearing the runaway champion.

Even as Lisa and Pepper caught up to the horse and pulled in front of it, even as Lisa reached for the reins, which flapped wildly around the horse's neck, the only thing Lisa could see in her mind's eye was Trudy's foot dangling dangerously through the stirrup.

Lisa reached down and grabbed Topside's reins with her right hand, holding her own in her left. As soon as Topside felt the first pressure from his reins, he slowed.

"Whoa there, boy," Lisa said in a low voice. His ears flicked toward her. "Ho up, there now," she told him. He came to an abrupt halt.

The stop was so abrupt that Trudy lost whatever semblance of balance she still had and nearly fell out of the saddle. Her grip on the horse's mane saved her.

"Is it over?" she asked in a shaky voice.

"It's over," Lisa told her. She took a deep breath, trying to be matter-of-fact. "Now get your feet in the stirrups, hold on to the reins, and let's get back to the stable."

"Do I have to ride?" Trudy asked. "Can I walk?"

"Did you ever hear the one about getting right back on the horse?" Lisa responded.

"Sure, but I never fell off." Trudy grinned impishly. "And besides that, I don't have to prove anything to myself. I know already that riding's not for me."

Lisa smiled. "You did fine, Trudy, you really did. An awful lot of riders wouldn't have handled that anywhere near as well as you did."

"I did?"

"Yeah, you did. Now let's go back. We can talk as we ride. I have some things to say to you."

Trudy took the horse's reins, adjusted her feet in the stirrups, and gave Topside a little nudge to get him going. He looked around at her, then obediently he followed her instructions.

"He's a little ashamed of himself," Lisa explained. "He knows he was naughty. He probably even knows he put you in danger. He'll be good now. He's trying to say he's sorry." She paused. "I wish I could do it as easily because I owe you as much of an apology as Topside does."

Trudy didn't say anything then and Lisa was glad. She had a lot to say, and although she wasn't sure exactly how to proceed, she knew the words would come to her. She just hoped she'd be able to say what she wanted better than she'd been able to write it.

"I think I owe you at least two apologies. First of all, when you said all those things to me about neighbors and friends, I didn't understand what you were really saying. Now that I've hurt you by making my second mistake, I do understand it. Gossip isn't news. Just because somebody *says* something doesn't mean somebody should print it. I made a lot of people unhappy with those articles about the thefts. I really messed up, I know. I had no right to use my friends just to get a good angle for a newspaper story."

Trudy still didn't say anything, but she was listening and that was all Lisa could really ask for.

"That's the first part of the apology. The second is more complicated. I know you heard Veronica reading the stupid story I wrote about you. I couldn't believe how insulting it sounded when I heard her read it. I didn't mean it that way! I really didn't. What I wanted people to know is that you're a neat person. You're not like anybody I've ever known before—and that's okay, but I guess that wasn't what I wrote because when Veronica read it out loud, it sounded awful. I'm sorry. I'm really sorry. I don't know what I can do to make it up to you."

"There's only one thing," Trudy said. "Only one way you can make it up to me."

"Yeah, what is it? I'll do it," Lisa promised.

"You did it already. You saved my life."

Trudy put her hand up for a high five. Lisa gratefully clapped her hand against Trudy's.

"Friends?" Lisa asked.

"Sure," Trudy agreed. "Unless being your friend means I have to ride horses."

Obviously, her recent experience had not made Trudy horse crazy.

"I think being friends means letting each other be themselves. I won't try to make you into a preppy country girl who rides if you won't make me into a funky punky city slicker."

"No way," Trudy said. "Day-Glo orange isn't your color!"

Lisa laughed. It was the first time she'd laughed in a while. It felt very good.

12

"Do my eyes deceive me?" Stevie asked Carole. The two of them were standing in Samson's paddock. They were trying not to move because they didn't want to encourage the colt to run.

"Stay still," Carole said.

"I can't," said Stevie. "If you'll turn very slowly, you'll see Trudy and Lisa riding in from the field trail together. It looks a lot like they're laughing together, like they're having fun together."

"You mean, like they're speaking to one another?" Carole asked.

"See for yourself."

Carole turned slowly. It was just as Stevie had said. "I don't believe it!"

Samson stepped toward Carole. She stood motionless except to open her hand enough for Samson to spot the sweet baby carrot she held in her hand. He sniffed tentatively and stepped closer, much more interested in the carrot than in the halter and lead rope that hung across her wrist. She patted him with her other hand. He stood still, waiting. She offered him the halter. He sniffed that curiously. She broke the carrot in two and gave him half. As he munched, she put the halter on him. He barely seemed to notice. This was his first carrot, and to Samson, that was much more interesting than the halter. Carole gave him the second half of the carrot. He lipped it up eagerly.

Samson was so busy with his newest experience that he simply forgot to notice the halter. He swallowed the final taste and looked at Carole for some more. She patted him.

"More carrot?" Stevie asked.

"No," Carole said. "This is a one-carrot lesson. See, we want him to learn about the halter more than about the carrots. Give the other carrot to Delilah."

Stevie offered it to the mare, who chomped on it noisily. Samson stayed near Carole. She suspected that his motive had more to do with carrots than trust, but she knew that trust would come in time.

Samson then realized he had a halter on. He shook his head. It didn't budge. He shook again.

"I'm going to leave it on a little longer this time," Carole said to Stevie. "I'd like it to stay on long enough for him to know for sure that it won't come off and it doesn't hurt. If we take it off too fast, he may conclude that it comes off when he shakes his head."

Carole slowly stepped over to the fence where Delilah's lead was fastened and where Stevie sat. She climbed up on the slatted boards and sat atop the fence next to Stevie. They watched the foal.

Samson continued shaking his head. He didn't seem angry or frightened, just curious and perhaps a little annoyed. When the halter didn't come off with shaking, he tried trotting around the paddock. That didn't work either. He nodded his head vigorously. Then he pranced around some more and came to the fence near Carole. There, he tried scraping it off his head by rubbing against the fence. Of course, that didn't work either.

Stevie smiled, watching him. "He's very funny, you know," she whispered to her friend.

"Yeah, I know," Carole whispered back, smiling at his antics. They didn't want to make loud sounds and startle the colt. "And I think I'm in love."

"I think he may be a little too young for you, Carole," Stevie quipped.

Samson was now staring at Carole, as if he realized for the first time that she was the one who had placed this mysterious thing on him. And that she was the one who could take it off. Carole didn't move.

"Isn't it time?" Stevie asked.

"Give it a minute more," Carole said, relaxing on the fence top. "I have a hunch it's time for lunch."

Delilah shifted her weight. The movement caught Samson's attention. He looked at his mother, then he looked at her udder. He hesitated a second, shaking his head one more time, but hunger overcame annoyance. He stepped forward, lowered his head, and began to nurse.

"Wonderful!" Carole said. "See, he's already comfortable enough to nurse with the halter on."

"Or else he's so hungry, he doesn't care."

"It doesn't matter which. The fact is he's doing it."

Lisa and Trudy joined them at the fence.

"He's so cute," Trudy observed.

"I thought you hated horses," Lisa teased.

"I do. But, he's not a horse. He's a foal or a colt—*not* a pony. He'll be a horse when he grows up, but for now, he's just a baby and that means he's cute."

"Nice work," Lisa said, pleased that Trudy actually remembered the things she'd said to her so long ago about Samson.

"Where have you guys been?" Stevie asked. "We missed you at class."

Lisa and Trudy exchanged glances. "We were on a little trail ride," Lisa explained. "Trudy wanted to try a few new things."

This sounded very hopeful to Stevie, who had encouraged Trudy to try a faster gait than a walk on horseback. "Oh, did you try trotting?" she asked.

Trudy looked to Lisa for the answer. She didn't know one gait from another. "Did I trot?" she asked.

Lisa grinned at her. "Nope, you skipped that one," she said. "You went straight to the gallop."

Stevie and Carole stared at them wide-eyed. "Gallop?" Carole asked.

Lisa and Trudy nodded.

"I think you've got some explaining to do," Stevie said to Lisa.

"Okay," Lisa agreed. "We'll tell you the story at your pool later this afternoon."

It was going to be a tough afternoon for Lisa. Not only would she and Trudy have to tell their tale of Trudy's nightmarish ride on Topside, but Lisa would have the opportunity to apologize to both of her best friends. She hoped she wouldn't have to save their lives, too!

For the next few minutes, the girls turned their attention to Samson, who finished his snack and then began rubbing his halter up against the fence again.

"Enough," Carole announced, dropping down into the paddock softly. "Here, boy," she said, holding her hands low. Samson stepped over to her and stood still while she removed the halter. "Good boy," she said, patting him. Grateful for his freedom, he once again pranced around the paddock. Carole climbed the fence while Stevie released Delilah's lead rope.

"Now can we play games with him?" Stevie asked hopefully.

"Not yet," Carole said. "I think we can begin doing

it next week, though. The first game we'll teach him will be follow-the-leader—on a lead rope."

"Okay, all right," Stevie conceded. "You were right, and I'm sorry I caused so much trouble."

"That's okay," Carole said. "After all, that's what friends are for!"

All four girls started laughing, and they were still laughing together as they headed for the locker area.

When they had all finished changing shoes, Lisa realized that she'd never spoken to Mrs. Reg about observing the adult class. Mrs. Reg was in her office. Lisa didn't want to miss the chance.

"You all go on ahead," she said. "I'll follow in a few minutes. There's something I have to speak to Mrs. Reg about. And I'll also have to talk to Max. Save some water for me, okay?"

It was a hot, humid day—too hot to stand on ceremony about getting to a swimming pool. Stevie, Carole, and Trudy agreed to proceed.

THIS WASN'T AN easy day for Lisa. She'd be glad when it was over, but until it was over, there was a lot of work to do. Not only did she have to talk to Mrs. Reg about the adult class, but she also had to thank her for helping her, and apologize for all the things she'd written about Pine Hollow. In fact, it seemed to Lisa that the list of people she had to apologize to was very long. It included Max and everybody in her riding classes—

even Veronica diAngelo. She took a deep breath. It was time.

Max was in Mrs. Reg's office when she knocked on the doorjamb, and both mother and son invited her in.

"I owe you both gigantic apologies," Lisa began in a rush. "I was trying to do something good for me that would be good for you, too, but I just didn't think about what I was doing. I made it sound as if nothing and nobody was safe here. I'm sorry and I won't do it again." Lisa looked down at the floor. She couldn't bring herself to meet Max's gaze.

"We knew you were just trying to help," Max said.

"But it didn't work at all," Lisa said. "It didn't help Stevie or Carole and it didn't help you. It didn't even help me!" She smiled, in spite of herself. "The first thing that did help me was your story today, Mrs. Reg. I knew you were telling me I had to make amends. I'm doing that now. I'm also planning a story for my next column, comparing young riders' classes with the adults'. Can I do that, Max? Will you let me observe?"

"Sure," he said, smiling wryly. "As long as you don't write about individuals in the classes."

"You mean you don't think I should include any un-kind descriptions of particularly bad riders and tell the whole world who they are?"

"Something like that," Max said, now genuinely laughing.

"I think I've learned my lesson," Lisa assured the Regnerys.

Mrs. Reg checked the calendar and class schedule. There was a class the next day that would do well for both of them.

"Uh, thanks," Lisa said before she left. "Thanks a lot."

"I think we owe you some thanks," Max said. "Somehow Trudy Sanders convinced Red she had an okay to ride by herself. I'm grateful to you for going out and fetching her back. She wasn't in any trouble, was she?"

Lisa thought for an instant before she answered. If she told Max what had really happened, she'd get Red in trouble, plus Stevie probably because Trudy was her guest, and definitely Trudy. Everything had worked out all right in the end, so what difference did it make?

"No, everything was fine," Lisa said. "I caught her before she made a wrong turn and got lost or she might have been in trouble."

"Well, thanks," Max said.

Lisa had the feeling she'd just exercised some of her newfound knowledge about journalism as well as friendship. You had to sort through facts before you reported them. Not all facts are news. She felt good about herself, really good, for the first time all day.

Rummaging around in her purse, Lisa couldn't find her pad and paper to make a note of the adult class she'd visit tomorrow. She had to make a note to herself or she'd forget it for sure. If she couldn't write it, she could record it. She felt in the bottom of her backpack for the dictating machine, but it wasn't there either. Lisa felt an empty feeling in her stomach. That was a valuable machine that her father had loaned her. He'd be furious if she'd lost it, and she'd be paying for it with her allowance until she had gray hair!

Hurriedly, she dumped out everything in her backpack. She found some old pencils and a stale pack of chewing gum, but there was no sign of the dictating machine.

When had she used it last? she asked herself. She recalled sitting on the bench in the locker area, right before Trudy had come in, dictating Trudy's name to herself so she would remember to write the ill-fated column that had appeared in today's paper. She hadn't seen it since then, she was sure. She'd put it away in her cubby that day, but where was it now?

For a few nightmarish moments, Lisa considered the possibility that there *was* a crime wave at Pine Hollow. The same person who had stolen Stevie's wallet had come back for her dictating machine—or maybe the theft of the machine was purely for revenge!

Now frantic, Lisa got down on the floor to reexamine the inside of her cubby on the bottom row. The deep cubby appeared to be completely empty. She reached in as far as she could. All she could feel was bare wood and then the wall at the back. She scrunched down lower and extended her arm farther. Then she felt something. She felt the edge of a small metal case. It took all the stretching and reaching she could manage to grab hold of it. With a sigh of relief she pulled out the dictating machine. Somehow, it had gotten so far back in the cubby that it had gone off the back end of it and was wedged between the bottom shelf and the wall.

Grateful to have solved the problem, she dropped the machine into her backpack and headed for Stevie's. She'd had enough problems for one day!

13

"You don't have to say anything," Carole told the weary Lisa when she arrived at Stevie's. "Trudy has told us the whole story. And don't worry, nobody's mad at you. You did a fabulous job rescuing Trudy, and anyway, we knew you'd eventually see what was happening with Hoof Beat. After all, you're our friend so you've got to be pretty terrific, right?"

Lisa smiled gratefully. "Thanks. It's a good thing I've got friends like you because when you mess up the way I have, you really need them!"

Stevie tossed a half-inflated beach ball at Lisa. "Come *on*! Go put on your bathing suit. We've been waiting for you so we could have chicken fights!"

"I'll be right back," Lisa promised, grinning over at Carole and Trudy. She headed for Stevie's room where she could change.

Stevie, who had been lying on her stomach on her towel, abruptly sat up. Although she was relieved to see the end of Lisa's weird behavior, she realized that all her troubles were not solved. She put her elbows on her knees and cupped her chin in her hands with a sigh.

"There's still one really big problem left," she said to Carole, "and that's your dad's birthday money."

"Something will work out," Carole said.

"Nothing's going to work. I've tried everything!" Stevie said.

"You're such a pessimist," Carole teased.

"Since when are you such an optimist!" Stevie retorted.

"I'm a realist," Trudy interrupted. "A realist knows that if you work smart instead of hard, problems get solved."

Carole and Stevie looked at her and burst out laughing. "Okay, smarty, what's our next step?" Stevie asked.

"I don't know," Trudy told her. "I always know what to say. I don't have to know what to do." She rolled over to sun her other side and put on her lime-green and black mirrored sunglasses to indicate she was done with her pronouncements.

"Okay, so we'll let the realist sleep," Stevie said to Carole. "Here comes our resourceful journalist. Let's see if she has any ideas."

It was such a hot, sticky day that Lisa didn't even

pause to greet her friends before she walked straight into the pool. She felt the cool water refresh her, almost cleansing the difficult day from her. She ducked into the clear water and swam the entire length of the pool.

She emerged, shook her head to clear the water from her eyes and ears, blinked twice, and said, "That feels wonderful!" She pulled herself up out of the pool, wrung the excess water out of her hair, spread her towel out by her friends, and lay down, content to do nothing. Stevie, however, wasn't going to let her do nothing.

"Okay then, beg, borrow, or steal?" she asked.

"Huh?" Lisa mumbled, already feeling sleepy in the fierce sun.

"The fifteen dollars Carole needs for her dad's birthday present," Stevie explained.

"Hmmm," Lisa said, reaching for the suntan lotion. "You know, I might have a solution for this. Let me think a minute." She began thinking about the work she'd been doing for the paper. She had certainly hurt enough people with her thoughtlessness. It seemed only right that she reverse the process. After all, Mr. Teller was going to pay her fifteen dollars a week. The least she could do would be to give Carole one week's worth.

"Hey, I could—wait a minute," Lisa said. Suddenly, Lisa's mind did a hop, skip, and jump. "I might even have two solutions to this problem." She sat up and looked at her friends excitedly. "Because I think I smell a—" She paused, thinking.

"A rat?" Stevie supplied. Lisa shook her head.

"A skunk?" Carole suggested. Lisa shook her head again.

"Well, *what?*" Trudy demanded, peering at them over the top of her sunglasses.

"I smell fresh paint!" Lisa announced.

"Of course you do," Stevie said. "That's all any of us has smelled at the stable for the last few weeks. The place stinks all the time!"

"That's it!" Lisa said excitedly. "*The* answer."

"It's not an answer, it's a problem," Stevie said. "I can't wait until they're done. It's taking forever because they just keep working on little pieces every day. It took them nearly a week just to finish up the locker area."

"And that's exactly what I mean," Lisa said. "See, whenever you paint, you have to move furniture around. Then when you're done painting, you move it back. Mostly, people would never really notice that the stuff had been moved, unless, of course, something didn't get back where it belonged."

"I think I see what you're getting at!" Stevie said excitedly.

Carole and Trudy just looked confused. Stevie explained, "What Lisa's saying is that the stableboys have been painting the locker area for weeks, and every time they do it, they move things—like the cubbies. Stuff that may have been way back in the cubby might, just might, be jostled out the back and get stuck someplace where somebody might not find it!"

"Oh!" Carole said. "Wouldn't that be something!"

"It sure would, and I'm not about to wait until Tuesday to find out if it's true. Let's go right now!"

Stevie didn't have to say it twice. The pool would be waiting for them when they got back. The girls pulled on shorts and tees over their bathing suits in record time and headed for Pine Hollow.

The stable was a short walk from Stevie's house, and they covered the distance quickly, barely talking at all. They were each too excited about the possibility of getting Carole's money back.

"Back again so soon?" Max asked, watching the girls parade past his office door.

"We're here on a hunch," Stevie said mysteriously. He shook his head and picked up his copy of *Horse Show.*

The locker area was empty when they got there. The wall of cubbies looked the way it always did, pushed up against the freshly painted wall.

"Lisa, you and Trudy get that end. Carole and I will take this one. We should only need to move the cubbies about six inches to see if your theory is correct," Stevie commanded, taking charge.

Everybody followed instructions. The block of cubbies was about ten feet long and almost five feet high. It was also two feet deep.

"One, two, three . . ."

They tried to pick up the shelves. They didn't budge.

"This thing weighs a ton!" Carole said, speaking for all of them.

"It doesn't matter what it weighs," Stevie said. "I know we can move it."

"Ah, the pessimist turns optimist!" Trudy teased.

"Save your breath for lifting," Stevie suggested.

"Four, five, six . . ." Lisa said. No more success.

"Why don't we try moving one end out from the wall at a time," Carole proposed. "That way, we can get extra muscle working together."

It worked. Quickly, they shifted to the other end and repeated the process. They did it again and again until Lisa, the smallest and skinniest of the crew, could squeeze behind the cubbies. Her friends stood on the other side and waited.

"One riding glove," she announced, tossing a brown kid glove over to them.

"Won't Veronica's daddy be happy?" Stevie said with a smirk.

"Three riding crops." They flew over the top, too. Carole wiped the dust off them and put them in the bucket where the crops were kept.

"A set of keys."

"Meg's, of course," Stevie said.

"Some underwear—red with white stars on them!"

"I wondered what had happened to these!" Stevie

said, grabbing them quickly and stuffing them back into her own cubby. Carole and Trudy laughed at her.

"Anything else?" Carole asked.

"Just this," Lisa said, her voice muffled.

"What?" Stevie asked, watching the top of the cubbies expectantly for the next item.

"Oh, just this old red wallet with fifteen dollars in it!" Lisa peered around the cubbies, a light gleaming in her eyes.

"All *right*!" Stevie yelled.

"I can't believe it!" Carole said.

"It's true. Believe it," Lisa told her, giving the wallet to Stevie. "And wait a minute, there's some other stuff here, too. I mean like money," she said, once again disappearing behind the wall of cubbies. "Here's a dime and three quarters, two pennies, and a—get this, it's a silver dollar."

"It must be interest," Trudy joked.

Lisa emerged from behind the cubbies and handed the change to Stevie. "If it's interest, it's yours since it was your wallet." Stevie put the change in her wallet, along with her own penny and Carole's fifteen dollars.

"Okay, let's move the cubbies back and get out of here. Our pool party's still waiting to happen," Stevie said. "And now we really have something to celebrate!"

Together, the girls shoved the cubbies back against the wall. They all felt so good about Carole's money that moving the shelf back was a lot easier than it had been moving it out. They stowed the recovered objects into each owner's cubby.

"Well, that's that," Carole said, slapping the dust off her denim cutoffs. "The entire mystery is solved and everything's been found."

"Not everything," Stevie said. "We found the gloves, the keys, and the riding crops, but what about Anna's hat?"

Lisa recalled that Anna had mentioned the disappearance of her hat. She had a feeling about that, too. "I wonder if one of the painters found her hat and didn't know what to do with it," she said, thinking out loud.

On the wall facing the cubbies hung dozens of nearly identical black velvet riding hats. Since hats were required, any rider who didn't own a hat could select one from the stable's collection.

"The easiest place to lose a black velvet hat is in the middle of a bunch of black velvet hats, don't you think? If we start on one end and work toward the other, I think we'll find that one of these hats has Anna's name in it."

It took only a few seconds. Anna's hat had carefully been stored on a very high hook, usually reserved for adult-size hats. Anna's hat was put in her cubby, and the girls were ready to return to the swimming pool.

"Last one in is a rotten egg," Stevie said.

"Nope," Lisa corrected her. "Today, there are no rotten eggs. We're all perfect!"

"Right," Stevie said. "And if you believe that one . . ." Laughing, the four girls threw their arms around each other and headed out the stable door.

14

"You know, I love the city, but malls are great!" Trudy announced when Mrs. Atwood dropped all four girls off the following morning to buy Colonel Hanson's birthday present.

"You mean you don't have malls in the city?" Lisa asked.

"Nope," Trudy said. "We've got lots of really cool stores in the downtown shopping area of Washington, but it's really not the same. It's neat to have so many different stores all in one building!"

"So, if we can't get her to like the country because of horses, malls will do it!" Stevie said. "I can't believe you have to leave tomorrow—I'm going to miss you. It's been fun pretending I have a sister. Will you come out here next weekend and go to the mall with us?"

"You bet," Trudy said. "Anytime. Malls are great!"

She glanced over at a group of boys dressed in colorful surfer shorts and tees who were hanging out in front of a burger place. The girls giggled.

"Okay, gang, enough sight-seeing—we've got work to do!" Lisa said, leading the group in the direction of the vintage-record store.

On the way, they passed the earring store where Trudy had gotten her shell-casing earrings. They also stopped at the department store and Happy Feet, the junior shoe store.

At the Preppy Puppy store, the girls couldn't decide which puppy was cutest—a cocker spaniel, a husky, or a spotted dalmatian—but they had fun cuddling them all!

Carole laughed as an overeager Yorkshire terrier covered her face with wet licks. "He's definitely cute," Carole said as she handed him back to the saleslady. "But not nearly as cute as Samson," Carole added to Stevie.

The Saddle Club practically had to drag Trudy out of the store. "Your apartment probably doesn't allow pets," Lisa reminded Trudy sympathetically.

After stopping for a soda, they went to the Scent Shop, where they sprayed themselves with a wild variety of perfumes.

"I think we smell worse than fresh paint," Stevie remarked, waving her hands in the air as they left the Scent Shop.

"I'm beginning to think the smell of paint is wonderful," Carole said. "After all, that was what gave Lisa the clue about where your wallet was."

"Okay, I love it, too. What's next?" Stevie glanced around the mall, looking for inspiration. "Look, over there!" She pointed to a makeup counter where they were offering free samples. "Trudy can show you how to do outrageous makeup on your eyes, right, Trudy?"

"Sure," she agreed. "But I don't know if they'll learn the butterflies as quickly as you did."

Lisa would never have imagined herself with eye shadow shaped like a butterfly, but when Trudy was done, she rather liked the effect. It was certainly different! "The new me?" she asked her friends, batting her eyelashes at them. They laughed and she did, too. "Well, anyway, I think I like my butterflies at least as much as Carole's rainbows!"

Lisa glanced at Carole and grinned. "Uh-oh, what's Stevie up to now?"

Stevie was intently staring into the countertop mirror as she drew a heart on her cheek with a red lip pencil. "Ta da!" she announced, spinning around from the counter.

"Cool," Trudy said with approval.

"I knew you'd like it. So, what's next?" Stevie asked. "I think that's my favorite question today."

"Well, you've done a good job of answering it," Lisa said. "I don't think I've ever had more fun without spending any money at the mall."

"So then it's time to spend. Here's the oldies record store," Carole said, leading her friends inside.

It always took Carole a long time to choose. Lisa and Stevie knew better than to help. This was too important to rush or to interfere with. Carole really wanted to be left alone on this job.

Stevie was eager to have more adventures, and Lisa and Trudy were willing to explore. They decided to leave Carole alone and come back to pick her up a half hour later. Carole was so intent on her mission that she barely acknowledged Stevie's suggestion.

"You know what I want to do?" Stevie said. "Remember the silver dollar you found?"

"Yeah," Lisa said, still feeling a little sheepish over their discovery of the Pine Hollow "thief."

"I want to find the place where they're selling raffle tickets for that library fund-raiser and I want to buy a raffle ticket. That's how I want to spend that dollar. I just have the feeling it's a lucky one."

"Okay," Lisa and Trudy agreed. The tickets were being sold at the small branch library in the mall. The girls had to pass seventeen tempting shops to get there. Since they only had a half hour, they didn't stop at any of them. Stevie felt very proud of that.

"Just one chocolate-covered pretzel?" Trudy begged as they passed Sweet Nothings.

"Maybe on the way back," Stevie graciously conceded. "We've got a mission to accomplish."

Lisa elbowed Trudy and grinned. "When Stevie's got a mission, that's when you've got to watch out!"

Stevie just stuck out her tongue and led the way up the escalator.

But when they got to the library branch, the usual card table for raffle ticket sales was gone.

"It must be over," Lisa said.

"No way—not until they have my silver dollar," Stevie said. "I'm going inside to ask."

Lisa and Trudy followed her inside.

Stevie loved the library. It was cool inside with subdued lights, nothing glaring or distracting. The whole place smelled of paper and bindings. It was filled with books that told wonderful stories and adventures of faraway places. Normally, she headed right for the animal-story section when she walked into the library, but not today. Today, she had another mission. The librarian was at the check-out desk.

"The raffle," Stevie said. "Is it too late?"

"Oh, I'm afraid so," the woman said. "We had the drawing last week. We're still trying to notify the prize winners. We'll take donations anytime, of course, but there aren't any more tickets."

Stevie pulled out her silver dollar. A silver dollar was a little special. Some people kept them as good-luck charms, she knew, but money in any form wasn't something Stevie could keep around for very long! Since a silver dollar *was* special, it needed to be used for something special. Even though she couldn't buy a raffle ticket, she had wanted the library to have the money. She decided to give it to them.

"Here, then," Stevie said. "You can have this."

"Why, thank you!" the librarian said, surprised and pleased. "And then next year, you come earlier and you can get some raffle tickets. Maybe you'll be as lucky as our grand prize winner."

"Who's that?" Stevie asked. "Someone from Willow Creek?"

"No, she doesn't live around here. I think she was just visiting. Somebody by the name of Trudy Sanders. We haven't been able to get ahold of her yet, but—"

"Did you say Trudy Sanders?" Stevie asked.

The librarian checked on a piece of paper on her desk. "Trudy Sanders, that's right," she said.

Stevie could feel the excitement rising in her. "And what did she win?" she asked.

"Oh, the grand prize is two weeks at Moose Hill Riding Camp. We need to find her soon. The camp starts in a week!"

"You've found her!" Stevie announced.

Excitedly, she signaled Lisa and Trudy to come to the counter and learn the good news. Stevie was too excited to speak.

Stevie and Lisa couldn't believe what incredible good luck Trudy had. They all shrieked with joy and hugged each other, jumping up and down. Usually, the librarians would make them leave for making such a ruckus, but since Trudy was the library's grand prize winner, they watched the girls with pleased smiles.

As soon as they'd gotten all the paperwork and the

certificate for the camp, the girls dashed out of the library and ran all the way to the record store. They found Carole just finishing up at the check-out counter.

It took only a few minutes to share Trudy's good news with Carole, but it took longer to convince her that it was true.

"This calls for a Saddle Club meeting to celebrate!" Lisa announced. "And I've gotten enough money from *The Gazette* to buy everybody a sundae!"

The four girls found an ice-cream shop that had exotic enough flavors to suit Stevie's weird taste. They found an empty booth and sat down.

"Hey, now that you're going to riding camp, you can be in The Saddle Club," Stevie said to Trudy while the waiter took their orders.

Trudy fiddled with her yellow parrot earrings. Then when the waiter had left to get them water, she said, "Look, I'd love to be in your club, but . . ." She paused, then looked across at Stevie. "I know you guys love horses. I'm sure they're great and they sure are pretty to look at, but they're just not my thing. Riding on the trail was okay. But riding along the river with Topside freaking out wasn't exactly a dream come true."

"But you were great. Lisa said so," Carole reminded her. "You just had an unusually bad experience. If you put your mind to it, you'll be a good rider."

"That's just the thing," Trudy explained. "I don't

want to put my mind to it. I really like you guys. And I'm glad we got to be friends. I'd like to visit again and I want you to come see me when you're in the city. But horseback riding? I'd rather wear plaid pants and turtlenecks!"

Stevie grinned. "You're going to have an awful time at Moose Hill then," she said.

"Oh, I would, if I were going, that's for sure," Trudy said. "But I'm not going."

"You're not?" all three Saddle Club girls said in a single voice.

"Of course not. Get real." The three friends laughed. "I want you to go in my place, Stevie. It's just a little thank-you for a really great visit with you."

All three girls turned to Stevie, who couldn't speak because her jaw had dropped.

When she could finally move and talk once again, Stevie did three things. First, she shrieked. Second, she hugged Trudy. And third, she had a proposal for Lisa.

"When we finish our sundaes, if you have any money left over, let's go back to the library and trade your dollar for the lucky silver dollar I gave them. I have the funny feeling we're going to need it to find a way for you and Carole to come to Moose Hill, too. I just can't see myself riding for two weeks without you two!"

Lisa and Carole agreed. The more The Saddle Club

stuck together, the more impossible it seemed that they could ever be apart.

"Here's to The Saddle Club at Moose Hill," Trudy announced, lifting her water glass in a toast.

The Saddle Club raised their glasses, too. "And here's a toast to our one nonriding, nonhorse-crazy, but definitely very cool member," Carole said, welcoming Trudy into their group.

Trudy grinned happily at her three new friends. She was as happy to be a part of their club as they were to have her.

"There's just one requirement," Trudy said to Stevie.

"Anything!" Stevie shouted.

"You've got to send me a postcard from camp. I want to hear about *everything*!"

ABOUT THE AUTHOR

BONNIE BRYANT is the author of more than thirty books for young readers, including the best-selling novelizations of *The Karate Kid* movies. The Saddle Club books are her first for Bantam Skylark. She wrote her first book six years ago and has been busy at her word processor ever since. (For her first three years as an author, Ms. Bryant was also working in the office of a publishing company. In 1986, she left her job to write full-time.)

Whenever she can, Ms. Bryant goes horseback riding in her hometown, New York City. She's had many riding experiences in the city's Central Park that have found their way into her Saddle Club books—and lots that haven't!

The author has two sons, and they all live together in an apartment in Greenwich Village that is just too small for a horse.

Great FREE offer just for you!

Join SNEAK PEEKS™!

Do you want to know what's new before anyone else? Do you like to read great books about girls just like you? If you do, then you won't want to miss SNEAK PEEKS™! Be the first of your friends to know what's hot ... When you join SNEAK PEEKS™, we'll send you FREE inside information in the mail about the latest books ... *before they're published!* Plus updates on your favorite series, authors, and exciting new stories filled with friendship and fun ... adventure and mystery ... girlfriends and boyfriends.

It's easy to be a member of SNEAK PEEKS™. Just fill out the coupon below ... and get ready for fun! It's FREE! Don't delay—sign up today!